BEFORE HE LAPSES

(A MACKENZIE WHITE MYSTERY—BOOK 11)

BLAKE PIERCE

D1528119

ISBN: 978-1-64029-613-8

PROLOGUE

Christine had only seen snow once before in her life. So when it started to come down around her as she made her way home from her boyfriend's house, she smiled. She figured that if she hadn't drunk so much tonight, she'd be able to enjoy it better. She was twenty years old but could not help but stick her tongue out to catch a few flakes. She chuckled under her breath at the feel of it...plus the fact that she'd come a long way from her home in San Francisco.

She'd transferred to Queen Nash in Maryland with a desire to focus on political science. Winter break was nearing its end and she was currently looking forward to dominating the coming spring's course load. It was one of the reasons she and her boyfriend, Clark, had been hanging out tonight—for one last hoorah before the semester began. There had been a little party of sorts and Clark, as usual, had too much to drink. She'd decided to walk home, just three blocks away, rather than stay there and have Clark's friends hit on her while their girlfriends shot her nasty looks. That's usually how any get-together at Clark's place ended when it didn't go the whole way with her going to his bedroom.

Besides...she was feeling overlooked. Clark was terrible about that, always choosing work, school, or getting drunk over her. There was someone else she could call when she got back to her apartment. Sure, it was late, but he had made it very clear that he was available for her at all hours. He'd proven it before, so why not tonight?

As she crossed a street between two blocks, she took note of how the snow was already sticking to the sidewalks. The storm had been expected so the roads had been treated and salted, but the white blanket of falling snow adhered to the sidewalks and the small strips of grass in front of and between the apartment buildings she passed.

By the time Christine reached her apartment, she almost decided to go back to Clark's place. It was cold and the snow was sending a little surge of childlike wonder through her. As she reached for her key to unlock the door to the apartment building, she nearly turned around and did just that.

The only thing that convinced her otherwise was knowing that she would not sleep well if she went back. Her own bed awaited her here, her warm blankets and at least a solid eight hours of sleep.

She walked inside and headed for the elevators. She pushed the three button and waited for the elevator to arrive. She was not drunk, just a bit tipsy, and she started to toy with the idea of having one more glass of wine when she got to her apartment and then making a call...to the man she'd been sort of seeing on the side for the last few months.

This was what was on her mind when the elevator arrived. She stepped on and took it up to her floor, liking the way her buzzed head felt as the elevator shifted upward.

She stepped off into her hall and found it empty. This made sense, as it was after one o'clock on a Wednesday night. She approached her door and again pulled her keys out. As they jostled in her still-cold hands, a voice from behind her gave her a jump.

"Christine?"

She turned at the sound of her name. She smiled when she saw him standing there. She wasn't going to have to call him after all. It was like he had anticipated her wanting him. It had been about a week or so, after all.

"Hey," she said.

He walked closer to her, his stride purposeful. He was looking at her in the way he usually did, with a fire in his eyes that made it clear what he wanted. The look alone turned her on—that, and the fact of who he was. He was off limits. He was...well, he was sort of dangerous, now wasn't he?

They met at her door, practically crashing into one another. The kiss was a little clumsy because it was so fierce. Her hands started exploring instantly. She grabbed the waist of his pants, pulling him closer. His hand traced the edges of her body, sliding down between her thighs as they clung to one another in the hallway.

"Inside," she managed to say between the kiss and her already heated breath. "Now."

She unlocked the door as he nibbled at her neck. She moaned, on edge for what was about to happen. She didn't even know if she'd be able to make it to the bedroom. Maybe not even the couch. The door unlocked and she pushed it open. When he came instantly to her, kicking the door closed, she pushed him away. She leaned back against the small kitchen counter and removed her shirt. He liked it when she undressed for him. It was a weird control thing, making him feel like she was serving him even before the sex started.

2

When she pulled her top up over her head, already reaching for the clasps of her bra, she looked into his eyes…and froze. He was standing still, that fire in his eyes gone now. Now, there was something else. Something new…something that scared her.

He cocked his head, as if examining her for the first time, and then he was on her. He'd been rough with her before, but this was new. This was not sexual in any way. He pressed his full weight against her and wrapped his hands around her neck. There was nothing playful about it; his grip was fierce, and she could feel her windpipe being squeezed right away.

It took less than ten seconds for her lungs to start to panic. When they did, she slapped at him furiously even as she felt her knees giving out.

She felt her chest growing tighter, as if there was some sort of force inside of her that was pushing the air out. When she fell to the floor, the back of her head struck the kitchen counter. His hands never left her neck, seeming to grow tighter and tighter the weaker she got.

She gave one final slap, but it was so weak that she wasn't even sure if it landed. When she hit the floor, he was on top of her. He continued to choke her, pressing his excited manhood against her. Her hands flailed for something—for anything—but all they found was the shirt she had just removed for him.

She barely had time to wonder why he was doing this before the darkness came rushing forward, relieving her of that terrible pain in her chest.

CHAPTER ONE

Mackenzie was standing in her bathroom, leaning against the sink and looking at the toilet. She'd looked at the toilet a lot lately, riding out her first trimester in a way that was almost *too* by-the-book. Her morning sickness had been particularly bad between weeks eight and eleven. But even now, as she was about halfway through week fifteen, it tended to be rough. She didn't have it nearly as often now but when it did hit, it was nasty.

She had already thrown up twice this morning and her stomach was hinting at a third time. But as she sipped some water and did her best to steady her breaths while bracing against the sink, she felt the third wave start to recede.

Mackenzie looked down at her stomach and placed her hand lovingly along the area that had just barely started to protrude over the last week or so. "Those are my intestines, little one," she said. "Not a foot rest."

She exited the bathroom and stood in the doorway for a moment, making sure she was done. When she felt that she had control of herself, she went to the closet and started getting dressed. She could hear Ellington in the kitchen, the clinks from the cupboard leading her to believe he was pouring coffee. Mackenzie would have loved a cup of coffee but as her luck would have it, it was one of the foods that the baby did not agree with when these episodes hit.

As she put on her pants, she noticed they were fitting a little more snug. She figured she had another month or so before she'd need to look into maternity clothes. And it would be around that time, she supposed, that she was going to have to tell Director McGrath that she was pregnant. She hadn't told him yet out of fear of how he might react. She was not quite ready to do nothing more than ride a desk or pull research duty for some other agent.

Ellington came to the doorway with a frown. He was indeed holding a cup of coffee. "Feeling any better?" he asked.

"Get that coffee out of here," she said. She tried to sound playful but it had come out a little bitterly.

"So, my mom keeps calling, wanting to know why we still haven't settled on a location for the wedding."

"Does she understand that it's not *her* wedding?" Mackenzie asked.

"No. I don't think she does understand that."

He stepped out of the room for a moment to set the coffee down and then came over to Mackenzie. He dropped to his knees and kissed her stomach as she searched for a shirt to wear.

"You still don't want to know the sex?" he asked.

"I don't know. Not right now, but I'll likely change my mind."

He looked up at her. From his position on the floor, he looked like a small child, looking up to a parent for approval. "When do you plan on telling McGrath?"

"I don't know," she said. She felt silly standing there half-dressed while he pressed his face against her stomach. Still, it also made her realize that he was here for her. He'd asked her to marry him *before* the baby and now, faced with an unexpected pregnancy, he was still here with her. To think that he was the man she would likely spend the rest of her life with made her peaceful and content.

"You afraid he'll sideline you?" Ellington asked.

"Yes. But another week or two and I don't think I'll be able to hide this baby bump."

Ellington chuckled and kissed her on the stomach again. "That's one sexy baby bump."

He kept kissing her, each one languishing a bit. She laughed and playfully tore herself away from him. "No time for all of that. We've got work. And, if your mother won't shut up, a wedding to finally plan."

They'd looked at venues and had even started to look into caterers for what they planned to be a small reception. But neither of them could really get into the flow of it. Through it all, they were finding that they had a lot in common: an aversion to all things fancy, a fear of dealing with organization, and an affinity to put work above all else.

As she got dressed, she wondered if she was cheating Ellington out of the experience somehow. Was her lack of enthusiasm toward planning the wedding making him think she didn't care? She hoped not, because that was not the case at all.

"Hey, Mac?"

She turned back to him as she started buttoning up her shirt. The nausea had mostly passed now, leading her to believe that she'd be able to tackle the day without any further ordeals. "Yeah?"

"Let's not plan it. Neither of us wants to. And really, neither of us wants a big wedding. The only person upset would be my mother and, quite frankly, I think I'd enjoy seeing that."

A smile crossed her face but she bit it back as quickly as she could. She'd like to see that as well.

"I think I know what you're saying. But I need you to say it, just to be sure."

He came back across the room to her and took her hands in his. "I'm saying I don't want to plan a wedding and I don't want to wait to marry you anymore. Let's just elope."

She knew he was being authentic because of the way his voice started to catch halfway through his comment. Still…it seemed too good to be true.

"Are you for real? You're not just saying it because…"

She stopped here, unable to finish the question, looking to her stomach instead.

"I swear to you it isn't just that," Ellington said. "While I'm very excited about raising and potentially scarring a kid with you, it's you I want right now."

"Yeah, we *are* going to scar the hell out of this kid, aren't we?"

"Not on purpose." He drew her close and hugged her. He then whispered in her ear and hearing his voice that close to her made her feel comfortable and content all over again. "I mean it. Let's do it. Let's elope."

She was nodding in agreement before they broke the hug. When they *were* face to face again, both of them had little glistening hints of tears in their eyes.

"Okay…" Mackenzie said.

"Yeah, okay," he said, a little giddy. He leaned in, kissed her, and then said: "So what do we do now? Shit, I guess there's still planning no matter which way we go here."

"We need to call the courthouse to book a time, I would think" Mackenzie said. "And one of us needs to get in touch with McGrath to ask for the time off for the ceremony. *Not it!*"

"Damn you," he said with a smile. "Fine. I'll call McGrath."

He took out his phone, meaning to do it right there and then, but then pocketed it. "Maybe this is a conversation I should have face-to-face with him."

She nodded, her arms trembling a bit as she finished buttoning her shirt. *We're going to do this,* she thought. *We're really going to do this…*

She was excited and nervous and elated, all of those emotions stirring within her all at once. She responded in the only way she could—by walking back over to him and taking him in her arms. And when they kissed, it only took about three seconds for her to decide that maybe there *was* time for what he had tried to start moments before.

***

The ceremony was two days later, on a Wednesday afternoon. It lasted no more than ten minutes and it ended with them exchanging the rings they had helped one another pick out the day before. It was so easy and carefree that Mackenzie wondered why women put themselves through the hell of all of that planning and scheduling.

Because at least one witness was needed, Mackenzie had invited Agent Yardley to attend. They had never really been friends, but she was a good agent and, therefore, a woman whom Mackenzie trusted. It was in asking Yardley to fill the role that she was once again reminded that she really didn't have any friends. Ellington was the closest thing to it and as far as she was concerned, that was more than enough.

As Mackenzie and Ellington came out of the courtroom and into the main hallway of the building, Yardley gave them her best effort at an encouraging parting speech before heading out quickly.

Mackenzie watched her go, wondering why she was in such a rush. "I won't say that was rude or anything like that," Mackenzie said, "but it looked like she could not wait to get out of here."

"That's because I spoke with her before the ceremony," Ellington said. "I told her to haul ass when we were done."

"That was rude. Why?"

"Because I convinced McGrath to give us until next Monday. I took all the time and stress I would have put into planning a wedding into planning a honeymoon."

"What? Are you kidding me right now?"

He shook his head. She wrapped him up in a hug, trying to remember a time when she had been this happy. She felt like a little girl who had just gotten everything she wanted for Christmas.

"When did you manage to do all of that?" she asked.

"Mostly on company time," he said with a smile. "Now, we have to hurry. We have bags to pack and sex to have. Our plane leaves in four hours for Iceland."

The destination sounded strange at first but then she remembered the "bucket list" conversation they'd had when she discovered she was pregnant. What were some things she wanted to get done before they brought a child into the world. One of Mackenzie's items had been to camp beneath the northern lights.

7

"Yeah, then let's go," she said. "Because with the way I'm feeling right now and the things I plan to do to you when we get back home, I don't know that we're going to make it to the airport on time."

"Yes ma'am," he said, hurrying her toward the door. "One question, though."

"What's that?"

He grinned at her and asked: "Can I call you Mrs. Ellington now?"

Her heart nearly leaped as he asked. "I suppose you can," she said as they headed out the door, entering the world for the first time as a married couple.

CHAPTER TWO

Murder had not been at all what he had expected. He had thought there would be some degree of *what have I done?* Maybe a moment of life-defining guilt or a sense that he had somehow altered the entire course of a family's life. But there had been none of that. The only thing he had felt after the murders—after killing both of his victims—was an overwhelming sense of paranoia.

And, if he was being honest, joy.

Perhaps he had been stupid to go about it so casually. He had been surprised by just how normal it had felt. He'd been terrified about the idea until he actually put his hands to their necks—until he squeezed down and robbed the life right out of their beautiful bodies. The best part had been watching the light go out in their eyes. It had been unexpectedly erotic—the most vulnerable thing he had ever seen.

The paranoia, though, was worse than he could have ever imagined. He had not been able to sleep for three days after he'd killed the first one. He had prepared for such an obstacle after the second, though. A few glasses of red wine and an Ambien directly after the murder and he had slept quite well, actually.

The other thing that was bothering him was how hard it had been to leave the scene of the crime the second time around. The way she had fallen, the way the life had gone out of her eyes in an instant…it had made him want to stay there, to stare into those freshly dead eyes to see what secrets might be in there. He'd never felt such a craving before, though to be fair, he would have never dreamed of killing anyone up until about a year or so ago. So apparently, much like taste buds, a person's morals were apt to change from time to time.

He thought about this as he sat in front of his fireplace. His entire house was quiet, so eerily still that he could hear the sound of his fingers moving against the stem of his wine glass. He watched the fire burn and pop as he drank from a glass of dark red wine.

This is your life now, he told himself. *You have killed not one but two people. Sure, they were necessary. You had to do it or your life might very well have been over. While neither of those girls technically deserved to die, it was all out of necessity.*

He told himself this over and over again. It was one of the reasons the guilt he had been expecting had not yet crippled him. It might also be why there was so much room for that paranoia to creep in and take root.

He was waiting for a knock at his door at any moment, with a police officer standing on the other side. Or maybe a SWAT team, complete with a battering ram. And the hell of it was that he knew he deserved it. He had no illusion about getting away with this. He figured that some day, the truth would be revealed. That's just the way the world worked now. There was no such thing as privacy, no such thing as living your own life.

So when the time came, he thought he'd be able to take whatever justice was dealt to him standing up like a man. The only question that remained was how many more would he have to kill? A small part of him begged him to stop, trying to convince him that his work was done now and that no one else had to die.

But he was pretty certain that was not true.

And worst of all, the prospect of having to go out and do it again stirred an excitement within him that shimmered and burned just like the fire in front of him.

CHAPTER THREE

She was very much aware that it was really only a change of setting that had done it, but sex in the Icelandic wilderness, right under the majestic swirl of the northern lights, was phenomenal. On the first night, when she and Ellington had wrapped up their festivities, Mackenzie slept better than she had in a very long time. She fell asleep happy, physically satisfied, and with the sensation of life growing inside of her.

They woke up the following morning and had very bitter coffee over a small fire at their campsite. They were in the northeastern part of the country, camping about eight miles away from Lake Mývatn, and she felt like they were the only people on the face of the planet.

"What would you say about fish for breakfast?" Ellington asked her out of the blue.

"I think I'm okay with the oatmeal and coffee," she said.

"The lake is only eight miles away. I can pluck a few fish out and have ourselves a real camping meal."

"You fish?" she asked, surprised.

"I used to do it a lot," he said. He got a faraway look in his eyes, one that she had long since learned meant that whatever he was talking about was a part of his past and likely tied to his first marriage.

"This I have to see," she said.

"Do I hear skepticism in your voice?"

She didn't say another word as she got to her feet and headed over to their rented four-by-four. "Fish sounds great," she said.

They piled into the four-by-four and made their way to the lake. Mackenzie enjoyed the open lands and the fjords, the countryside looking at times like something out of a fairytale. It was a stark contrast to the hustle and bustle she was growing accustomed to in DC. She looked over to Ellington as he drove them toward Lake Mývatn. He looked ruggedly handsome, his hair still slightly tousled from a night in the tent. And while they had plans to check into a small motel for the night, mainly just to get showers before returning to camp, she had to admit that there was something alluring about seeing him a little grimy, a little rough

11

around the edges. Seeing him like this somehow made it much easier to fathom the idea of spending the rest of her life with him.

They were at the lake twenty minutes later, Ellington sitting on a rickety old dock with a rented fishing pole in his hands. Mackenzie only watched him, the two of them sharing nothing more than small talk. She was enjoying the moment of seeing him doing something that she had not even *thought* he would enjoy. It only clued her in to the fact that there was so much more about him that she had to learn—a sobering thought while looking at the man she had married only two days ago.

When he brought in his first fish, she was very surprised. And by the time he had three on the dock, tossed in a small bucket, she was equally surprised in herself and the fact that she was rather attracted to this side of him. She wondered what other outdoorsy-type activities Ellington was good at that he had been hiding from her.

They rode back to the campsite, the Jeep smelling of the three fish that would be their breakfast. Back at the site, she saw that his fishing expertise stopped at taking them out of the water. He was a little clumsy in scaling and gutting them; although they did end up having some delicious fish over a campfire, it was in ragged, small morsels.

They made plans for the day, plans that included horseback riding, a waterfall tour, and a journey to the small motel outside of Reykjavík to shower and get a proper meal before driving back out through the gorgeous countryside to the campground as night fell. And after eating their breakfast of fresh fish, they carried that plan out step by step.

It was all very dreamlike and, at the same time, a very vivid way to start their life together. There were moments, holding him or kissing him amidst this incredible scenery, that she knew she would remember all throughout her life, perhaps down to her final breaths. She had never felt more content in her life.

They returned to their campsite, where they restoked the campfire. Then, freshly showered and with a good, full meal in their stomachs, they retired to the tent and made a *very* long night of it.

***

With just two days remaining in their honeymoon, they went on a private glacier tour along Iceland's Golden Circle. It was the only day of the trip where Mackenzie had been stricken with morning sickness and, as a result, opted out of their chance to go glacier climbing. She watched as Ellington took part, though. She enjoyed watching him tackle the task like an overeager child. It was a side of him she had seen here and there, but never to this extent. It then dawned on her that this was the most time they had ever spent together outside of work. It had been like some sporadic paradise and had opened her eyes to just how much she loved him.

As Ellington and the instructor started their descent down the glacier, Mackenzie felt her cell phone vibrating in her coat pocket. They had turned all sound off as they had gotten on their plane to start the honeymoon but, given their careers, had not allowed themselves to kill the phones completely. To occupy herself while Ellington came down from the glacier, she pulled the phone out and checked it.

When she saw McGrath's name on the display, her heart dropped. She'd been on an emotional high these last few days. Seeing his name made her believe that it was going to come to a pretty quick end.

"This is Agent White," she said. She then thought: *Damn...missed my first chance to refer to myself as Agent Ellington.*

"It's McGrath. How's Iceland?"

"It's nice," she said. And then, not caring that she was being a little too vulnerable with him, corrected herself. "It's amazing. Really beautiful."

"Well, then, you're going to hate me for calling, I'm sure."

He then told her why he was calling, and he was right. When she ended the call, she *was* quite upset with him.

Her hunch had been correct. Just like that, their honeymoon was over.

CHAPTER FOUR

The transition had been easy enough. The hurrying and rushing for their flight and then having to catch a red-eye back to DC made the magic of their honeymoon slowly dissolve back into the boundaries of real life. Mackenzie was quite pleased to feel some of that magic still existing between them, primarily in realizing that even here, back in the States and surrounded by their jobs, they were still married. Iceland had been magical, sure, but it had not been the only thing bonding them over those few days.

What she had not been expecting was just how prominent her wedding ring felt on her finger as she and Ellington walked into McGrath's office just fourteen hours after he had interrupted their honeymoon. She was not so naïve as to feel like it made her a new person, but she did see it as a sign that she had changed—that she was capable of growing. And if that was true in her personal life, then why not her professional life?

Maybe it will start once you tell your superior that you're currently fifteen weeks pregnant, she thought.

With that thought lodged in her head, she also realized that the case they had been called in for would likely be the last one before she had to come clean about her pregnancy—though the thought of trying to track down murderers with a baby belly did make her grin.

"I appreciate you two coming in early on this," McGrath said. "And I also want to congratulate you on your marriage. Of course, I don't like the idea of a married couple working together. But I want this one wrapped up very quickly, as there could be the potential for mass panic on a college campus if we don't get it wrapped very soon. And you two undeniably work well together, so here we are."

Ellington looked over at her and smiled at the last comment. Mackenzie was nearly disarmed at how strongly she felt for him. It was a beautiful thing but also made her a bit uncomfortable as well.

"The latest victim is a sophomore at Queen Nash University in Baltimore. Christine Lynch. She was killed in her kitchen very late at night. Her shirt had been removed and was found on the floor. She was very obviously strangled. From what I understand, there were no prints on her neck, indicating the killer was wearing gloves."

"So the murder was premeditated and not situational," Mackenzie said.

McGrath nodded and slid over three photos of the crime scene. Christine Lynch was a very pretty blonde and in the pictures, her face was turned to the right. She was wearing makeup and, as McGrath had said, her shirt had been removed. She had a small tattoo on her shoulder. A sparrow, Mackenzie thought. The sparrow seemed to be looking up toward the area where the bruising around her neck started; the bruising on her neck was obvious even in the photos.

"The first," McGrath said, opening up another folder, "was a twenty-one-year-old named Jo Haley. Also a Queen Nash student. She was found in her bedroom, in bed and completely naked. The body had been there for at least three days before her mother called to report suspicious activity. There were signs of strangulation but not quite as vicious as what we see on Christine Lynch. CSI found evidence of sexual activity just prior to her death, including an empty condom wrapper."

He slid the crime scene photos over to them. There were more pictures of Jo Haley, primarily the bruising around her neck from where someone had apparently strangled her. She, like Christine Lynch, was fairly attractive. She was also very thin, almost to the point of being waifish.

"So the only real lead we have is that two pretty girls from Queen Nash have been killed, probably during or just prior to sex?" Mackenzie asked.

"Yes," McGrath said. "Given the coroner's estimated time of death for Jo Haley, they were killed no more than five days apart."

"Do we have estimated times of the night they were killed?" Mackenzie asked.

"No. Nothing concrete, but we do know that Christine Lynch had been seen at her boyfriend's apartment up until about one in the morning on Wednesday. Her body was discovered by her boyfriend the following day when he went to her apartment."

Ellington studied the last of the pictures and slid them back to McGrath. "Sir, with all due respect, I'm a married man now. I can't just go approaching pretty young women on college campuses anymore."

McGrath rolled his eyes and looked at Mackenzie. "I wish you the best of luck with this," he said, nodding toward Ellington. "In all seriousness…I want this wrapped as soon as possible. Winter break is over next week and I don't want panic on campus as all of these students are returning from home."

As if swapping personalities at the flip of a switch, Ellington became all business. "I'll grab the case files and we'll get started right away."

"Thank you. And seriously…enjoy this case together. I don't think it's a good idea for you two to be working together now that you're married. Consider this case my wedding gift to the two of you."

"Really, sir," Mackenzie said, unable to help herself, "I would have much preferred a coffee maker."

She could barely believe it when the flicker of a smile spread across McGrath's lips. He bit it back right away as Mackenzie and Ellington headed out of his office with their first case as husband and wife and, subsequently, their final case as a team.

CHAPTER FIVE

Per Mackenzie's usual approach, they began with the scene of the most recent crime. It was the equivalent to looking over a warm body—the warm body much more prone to giving up clues or indications more so than a body that had been cold for a while. On the drive up to Maryland, Mackenzie had essentially read the case files out loud while Ellington drove.

When they arrived at Christine's apartment in Baltimore, they were met by a deputy from the local police department. He was an older gentleman, probably on his last year or two with the force and given clean-up on cases like this one.

"Good to meet you," he said, shaking their hands with the kind of good cheer that made him almost obnoxious. "Deputy Wheeler. I've been sort of overseeing this one."

"Agents White and Ellington," Mackenzie said, again realizing she still wasn't quite sure how to address herself. It was not something she and Ellington had discussed yet, although their marriage certificate did refer to her as Mackenzie Ellington.

"What can you tell us from your perspective?" Ellington asked as they stepped into Christine Lynch's apartment.

"Well, we got here, my partner and me, and met with the boyfriend and went in. She was right there, on the kitchen floor. Had her shirt off, laying on her side. Her eyes were still open. She was very clearly strangled and there were no signs of a struggle or anything like that."

"It was snowing on the night it happened," Ellington said. "Were there no wet footprints in the hallway?"

"No. From what we can gather, the boyfriend didn't come in until the following afternoon. Anywhere between ten and sixteen hours could have passed between the last time he saw her and the moment she was killed."

"So it was a clean scene, then?" Mackenzie asked.

"Yeah. No clues, no snowy or wet footprints. Nothing of any interest."

Mackenzie thought back over what she had read in the case files—particularly of a rather personal note the coroner had added to the file no more than six hours ago. In preparing the body for examination, they had found evidence of sexual arousal when removing Christine's underwear. This, of course, could have been the result of time spent with the boyfriend. But if she had been found here, with her shirt removed and in her kitchen…well, it pointed to the fact that maybe someone had met her here after she'd left her boyfriend's apartment. And maybe they hadn't wanted to take the time to make it to the bedroom.

"Did local PD ask to see security tapes?" Mackenzie asked. "I noticed at least two on the sides of the building when we were coming in."

"We've got someone working on that right now," Wheeler said. "Last I heard, which was about two hours ago, there's nothing of note on the footage. You're welcome to check it out for yourself, though."

"We may take you up on that," Mackenzie said as she left the kitchen and stepped into the living area.

Christine had lived a very neat life. Her small bookcase on the right side of the living room was neatly stacked and the titles, many of which were biographies and old political science textbooks, were alphabetized. There were a few pictures placed here and there on the two end tables and the walls. Most of them were of Christine and a woman who was clearly her mother.

She then moved to the bedroom and looked around. The bed was made and the rest of the room was just as proper as the living room. The few items that were displaced on her bedside table and desk revealed very little: pens, pocket change, an iPhone charger, a pamphlet for a local politician, a glass with just a swallow of water remaining in it. It was evident that nothing of a physical nature had occurred in this room on the night Christine had died.

It opened up many questions and conclusions, all of which Mackenzie sorted out in her head as she made her way back out into the kitchen.

Someone met her here when she returned from her boyfriend's apartment. Was she expecting them or did they surprise her?

The fact that her body was discovered inside the apartment and her shirt was off likely means that, expected or a surprise, she invited the killer in. Did she invite him in having absolutely no idea that she was in danger?

When she got back into the kitchen, Ellington was taking down notes as he spoke to Deputy Wheeler. She and Ellington exchanged a look and a nod. It was one of the many ways they had learned to fall into sync with one another on the job—a non-verbal language that saved many interruptions and awkward moments.

18

"Well, Deputy Wheeler, I think we're good here," Ellington said. "By chance, were you also placed on the Jo Haley murder from a few days ago?"

"No. But I know enough about the case to help if you need it."

"Great. We'll call on you if it comes to that."

Wheeler seemed pleased with this, smiling to them both as they left Christine Lynch's apartment. Outside, Mackenzie looked to the sidewalk, where there were only sparse indications that it had snowed at all. She smiled thinly as she realized that she and Ellington had likely been about to get married when this poor girl had died.

Christine Lynch won't ever have the privilege of a wedding or a husband, Mackenzie thought. It made her feel a pang of sorrow for the woman—a sorrow that deepened when she realized that there was another rite of womanhood that she would also never feel.

Wrapped in that sadness, Mackenzie placed a hand on her barely bulging stomach, as if protecting what was inside.

***

After a call to the bureau, Mackenzie and Ellington discovered that Christine's boyfriend was a twenty-two-year-old fellow Queen Nash student. He worked part-time with a public health office to get his feet wet for whatever career awaited him after graduating with his public health degree. They found him not at work, but at his apartment, apparently having taken the loss of Christine much harder than a typical boyfriend.

When they arrived at his apartment, Clark Manners was habitually cleaning what already looked to be a sparkling clean apartment. It was clear that he had not slept well recently; his eyes were glazed over and he walked as if some unseen force was having to push him along. Still, he seemed enthusiastic when he invited them into his apartment, eagerly wanting to get to the bottom of what had happened.

"Look, I'm not stupid," he said as they sat down in his immaculately cleaned living room. "Whoever killed her…they were going to rape her, right? That's why her shirt was off, right?"

Mackenzie had wondered this herself, but the crime scene photos told a different story. When Christine had fallen to the floor, she'd landed on the shirt. That seemed to indicate it had come off rather easily and had been discarded on the floor. If Mackenzie had to wager a bet, she'd bet that Christine had taken it off herself, likely for whomever she had invited in—whoever had ended up killing her. Plus...Mackenzie wasn't so sure the murderer had intended to rape Christine. If he'd wanted to, he could have. No...Mackenzie thought he had come by to kill her and that was all.

But this poor guy didn't need to know that.

"It's just too early to tell," Mackenzie said. "There are several different ways it could have gone down. And we were hoping you could maybe provide some insights to help us figure it all out."

"Sure, sure," Clark said, clearly in need of a long nap and less coffee. "Anything I can do, I'll do."

"Can you describe the nature of your relationship with Christine?" Ellington asked.

"We'd been dating for about seven months. She was the first real relationship I've ever had—first one that lasted more than two or three months. I loved her...I knew that after about a month."

"Had it reached a physical level yet?" Mackenzie asked.

With a faraway look in his eyes, Clark nodded. "Yeah. It got there pretty quickly."

"And on the night she was killed," Mackenzie said, "I understand that she had just come from here, from this apartment. Did she stay over often?"

"Yeah, once or twice a week. I'd stay over there sometimes, too. She gave me a key to just come and crash whenever a few weeks ago. That's how I was able to get into her place...that's how I found her..."

"Why did she not stay here that night?" Ellington asked. "It was late when she left. Was there an argument between the two of you?"

"No. God, we rarely argued about anything. No...we'd all been drinking and I had far too much. I kissed her goodnight while she was still out here with some of my friends. I went to bed and passed out, feeling a little sick. I was sure she'd eventually join me but when I woke up the next morning, she was gone."

"Do you think any of your friends might have given her a ride?" Mackenzie asked.

"I asked all of them and they said no. Even if they'd offered, Christine would have said no. I mean, it's only like three blocks and she likes the cold weather...likes to walk around in it. She's from California, so the snow is this cool magical thing, you know? I even remember...that night she was excited because there was snow in the forecast. She was joking about taking a walk out in it."

"How many friends were here with you that night?"

"Including Christine, there were six of us in all. From what I gather, they all left not too long after she did."

"Can we get their names and contact information?" Ellington asked.

"Sure," he said, pulling out his phone and starting to locate the information.

"Is it common for you to have that many people over on a weekday night?" Mackenzie asked.

"No. We were just sort of getting together for one last hoorah before winter break came to an end. Classes start next week, you know? And with work schedules and visiting family, it was the only time we could all get together."

"Did Christine have any friends outside of your group?"

"A few. She was sort of an introvert. There was me and then two of my friends that she hung out with, but that's about it. She was really close with her mother, too. I think her mom was planning to come out here before the end of the semester—like to move out here for good."

"Have you spoken with her mother at all since this all happened?"

"I did," he said. "And it was weird because it was the first time I ever spoke to the woman. I was helping her out with…"

He paused here, his tired eyes showing signs of tears for the first time.

"…with funeral arrangements. She's having her cremated here in town, I think. She flew in last night and she's staying at a hotel somewhere out here."

"Any family with her?" Mackenzie asked.

"I don't know." He hunched over and looked at the floor. He was both exhausted and sad, a mixture that looked to have finally devastated him.

"We'll leave you alone for now," Mackenzie said. "If you don't mind, do you have Mrs. Lynch's hotel information?"

"Yeah," he said, slowly pulling his phone back out. "Hold on."

As he pulled up the information, Mackenzie looked over to Ellington. As always, he was being hyperaware, looking around the place to make sure they weren't missing anything obvious. She also noticed, though, that he was tinkering with his wedding ring as he studied the place, turning it slowly around and around on his finger.

She then looked back at Clark Manners. She was pretty sure they may end up questioning him again—and probably soon. The fact that he was obsessively cleaning his house after his girlfriend's death made sense from a psychological standpoint but it could also be seen as an attempt to get rid of any evidence.

But she had seen people broken over grief before and she felt deep down in her gut that Clark was likely innocent. No one could fake this sort of grief and inability to get a good night's sleep. They may need to speak with some of his friends at some point, though.

As Clark found the information, he handed over his phone so Mackenzie could take it down. She also took down the names and numbers that Clark had pulled up for all of the friends that had been at his apartment on the night Christine was killed. As she took the information down, she realized that she had also been fidgeting with her wedding ring. Ellington had noticed her doing it, managing a quick smile at her in spite of the situation. She stopped rotating the ring when she took the phone from Clark.

***

Margaret Lynch was just about the exact opposite of Clark Manners. She was cool and collected, greeting Mackenzie and Ellington with a smile when they met with her in the lobby of the Radisson she was staying in. She led them to a couch near the back of the lobby, though, showing her first sign of weakness.

"If I end up crying, I'd rather not do it in front of everyone," she remarked, pressing herself into the couch as if she was fairly certain this would indeed happen.

"I'd like to start with asking how well you know Clark Manners," Mackenzie said.

"Well, I spoke to him for the first time two days ago, after all this had happened. But Christine had mentioned him a few times on the phone. She was quite taken with him, I think."

"Is there any suspicion on your part?"

"No. Of course, I don't know the boy but based on what Christine told me about him, I don't see him being the one who did this."

Mackenzie noted that Mrs. Lynch was doing everything she could to avoid words like *killed* or *murdered*. She figured the woman was able to keep her head because she was doing a good job of distancing herself from it. It was probably made easier by the fact that the two of them had been living on separate ends of the country for a while.

"What can you tell me about Christine's life here in Baltimore?" Mackenzie asked.

"Well, she started college in San Francisco. She wanted to be a lawyer, but the school and the course load…it wasn't a good fit. We had a long talk about her applying to Queen Nash University. A *long* talk. Her father passed away when she was eleven and really, it's just been Christine and I since then. No uncles, no aunts. It's always been a small family. She has one surviving grandmother, but she has dementia and is in a home out near Sacramento. I don't know if you know yet or not, but I'm having her cremated here, in Baltimore. No sense in going through the process of getting her back to California just to have the same thing done. We have no ties to the area, really. And I know she enjoyed it here, so…"

This poor woman is going to be all alone, Mackenzie thought. She was always aware of these sorts of things when interviewing and interrogating people, but this thought seemed to slam into her like a boulder.

"Anyway, she got in and within a single semester, she knew she loved it here. She was always very apologetic, worried that I was this lonely old woman living alone without her. She kept in touch, calling about twice a week. She'd tell me about how classes were going and, like I said, she ended up telling me about Clark."

"What did she say about him?" Ellington asked.

"Just that he was cute and very funny. She did mention from time to time that he wasn't very exciting and that he had a tendency to drink too much whenever they were in social situations."

"But nothing negative?"

"Not that I can remember."

"Please forgive me for asking," Mackenzie said, "but do you know if they were exclusive? Was there a chance Christine might have also been seeing anyone else?"

Mrs. Lynch thought about this for a moment. She didn't seem to take offense to the question; she remained just as calm as she had seemed when they had first come into the lobby and met her. Mackenzie wondered at what point the poor woman was going to eventually snap.

"She never mentioned any competition for her heart," Mrs. Lynch said. "And I think I know why you're asking. I was told what the scene looked like—her being topless and all. I had just assumed…"

She stopped here and took a moment to collect herself. The words that were coming next caused something to stir inside, but she managed to get it down before the emotions took over. When she resumed, she was still stone-faced.

"I had just assumed it was a rape gone wrong. That maybe the man got frustrated for some reason and wasn't able to go through with it. But I suppose there's a chance there was another man in her life. If there was, I just didn't know about it."

23

Mackenzie nodded. The would-be-rapist theory had gone through her head as well, but the way the shirt had been tossed to the floor and then her head haphazardly lying on it...none of it seemed to add up.

"Well, Mrs. Lynch, we don't want to bother you any more than we absolutely have to," Mackenzie said. "How long do you intend to stay in town?"

"I don't know yet. Maybe a day or two beyond the service." At the word *service*, her voice cracked the tiniest bit.

Ellington handed her one of his business cards as he got to his feet. "If you happen to think of anything or hear anything during the funeral or the services, please let us know."

"Of course. And thank you for looking into this." Mrs. Lynch looked forlorn as Mackenzie and Ellington left. *I suppose so,* Mackenzie thought. *She's all alone in a city she doesn't know, having come to take care of her deceased daughter.*

Mrs. Lynch saw them to the door and waved them off as they walked to their car. It was the first moment in which Mackenzie realized that her hormones were officially all over the place as a result of her pregnancy. She felt for Mrs. Margaret Lynch in a way she might not have before she'd found out she was pregnant. To create life, then raise and nurture it only to have it wrenched away from you in such a brutal fashion...it had to be miserable. Mackenzie felt absolutely wretched for Mrs. Lynch as she and Ellington pulled out into traffic.

And just like that, Mackenzie felt a flush of determination. She'd always had a passion for righting wrongs—for bringing killers and other evil men and women to justice. And whether it was hormones or not, she vowed to find Christine Lynch's killer, if for no other reason than to bring some closure to Margaret Lynch.

CHAPTER SIX

The first name on the list of friends Clark Manners had given them was a guy named Marcus Early. When they tried contacting him, the call went straight to voicemail. They then tried the second name on the list, Bethany Diaggo, and were able to set up an interview right then and there.

They met Bethany at her place of employment, a law firm where she was interning as part of her course load at Queen Nash. As the day was winding down to dinnertime, she simply clocked out half an hour early and met with them in one of the small conference rooms in the back of the building.

"We understand that you were at Clark Manners's apartment on the night that Christine was killed," Mackenzie said. "What can you tell us about that night?"

"It was just getting together to have some fun. We had a bit to drink—maybe a little too much. We played some card games, watched some reruns of *The Office,* and that was about it."

"So there were no arguments of any kind?" Mackenzie asked.

"No. But I did see that Christine was starting to get irritated with Clark. Sometimes when he drinks, he tends to go a little overboard, you know? She never said anything that night, but you could tell she was starting to get irritated."

"Do you know if it ever caused problems with them in the past?"

"Not that I know of. I think Christine just sort of dealt with it. I feel pretty sure that she knew their relationship wasn't this forever sort of thing."

"Bethany, did you know a woman named Jo Haley? About your age, also a Queen Nash student?"

"I did," she said. "Not quite as well as I knew Christine, but we were on a friendly basis. It was rare that we ever hung out. But if we crossed paths at a bar or something like that, we'd usually end up siting together and chatting."

"I assume you know that she was murdered several days ago as well?" Ellington asked.

"I did. In a very cruel twist of irony, it was actually Christine that broke the news to me."

"Do you know how she found out?" Mackenzie asked.

"No clue. I think they shared some of the same classes. Oh, and they had the same academic advisor, too."

"Academic advisor?" Ellington asked. "Is that just some fancy way of saying *guidance counselor*?"

"More or less," Bethany said.

"And you're certain Jo and Christine had the same one?" Mackenzie asked.

"That's what Christine said. She mentioned it when she told me Jo had been killed. She said it felt a little too close to home." Bethany paused here, perhaps understanding the eerie precognitive weight of the comment for the first time.

"Would you happen to have the name of this advisor?" Mackenzie asked.

Bethany thought for a moment and then shook her head. "Sorry. No. She mentioned it when we were talking about Jo, but I don't remember it."

No big deal, Mackenzie thought. *A quick call to the university will get that information for us.*

"Is there anything else about either Jo or Christine you might be able to tell us?" Mackenzie asked. "Anything that might give anyone reason to want them dead?"

"Nothing at all," she said. "It doesn't make any sense. Christine was very focused and drama free. It was all about school and trying to get an early start on her career. I didn't know Jo enough to really make a judgment there, though."

"Well, thank you for your time," Mackenzie said.

As they left the office and Bethany readied to leave for the day, Mackenzie tried to imagine these two dead women crossing paths in the hallways and concourses of the university. Maybe they passed by one another as one left their advisor's office while the other was walking toward an appointment. The idea of it was a little creepy but she knew far too well that things like this tended to happen quite often in murder cases where there was more than one victim.

"University offices are still closed for the holiday break," Ellington pointed out as they got back into the car. "Pretty sure they reopen tomorrow."

"Yeah, but I'd assume there's some sort of employee directory on the website. Based on some of the books I saw in Christine's apartment and some political literature in her bedroom, I think it's safe to assume she's a political science major. We could narrow it down that way."

Before Ellington was able to tell her what a good idea this was, Mackenzie was already on her cell phone. She opened up her web browser and started scrolling. She was able to find a directory, but, as she had assumed, there were no direct or personal numbers; they were all numbers to the advisors' offices. Still, she located the two different advisors that were assigned specifically to the political science department and left messages for each one, asking them to call her back as soon as they got the message.

As soon as she was done with that, she scrolled a bit more, this time through her contacts list.

"What now?" Ellington asked.

"There are only two of them," she said. "Might as well see if we can get some sort of a background check running on them—see if there are some red flags."

Ellington nodded, smiling at her quick train of thought. He listened to her as she placed the information request. Mackenzie could feel his eyes flitting over to her every now and then, a caring and watchful sort of stare.

"How are you feeling?" he asked.

She knew what he meant, that he was veering away from the case and asking about the baby. She shrugged, seeing no point in lying to him. "All of the books say that the nausea should be coming to an end soon, but I'm not believing it. I felt it a few times today. And, if I'm being honest, I'm pretty tired."

"So maybe you need to go back home," he said. "I hate to sound like that domineering husband type, but...well, I'd really rather you or my baby not get hurt."

"I know. But this is a series of murders on a college campus. I doubt it's going to get dangerous. It's probably just a testosterone-laced guy that gets his rocks off on killing women."

"Fair enough," Ellington said. "But will you be honest with me and tell me if you start to feel weak or just out of sorts?"

"Yes. I will."

He eyed her suspiciously, yet playfully, as if he wasn't sure if he should trust her. He then reached out and took her hand as he headed back toward the center of town to find a hotel for the night.

***

They'd barely had enough time to settle into their room when Mackenzie's phone rang. Ignoring the unfamiliar number, she answered it right away. She could feel the ticking clock McGrath had placed on them, ticking away second by second. She knew that

27

if this thing wasn't solved by the time classes started next week—in just five days, in fact—it would be increasingly harder to wrap up with all of the students back in the area.

"This is Agent White," she said, answering the call.

"Agent White, this is Charles McMahon, an academic advisor over at Queen Nash University. I'm returning a message you left for me."

"Great, and thanks for the promptness. Are you at the college right now?"

"No. I have a bit of a heavy workload right now, so I had all of my voicemail from the office rerouted to my personal phone."

"Oh, I see. Well, I was wondering if you might be able to answer a few questions about a recent murder."

"I assume it's about Jo Haley?"

"No, actually. There's been another murder, two days ago. Another Queen Nash student. A young woman named Christine Lynch."

"That's terrible," he said, sounding genuinely shocked. "Is it...well, with two women in such a short amount of time...do you think it's a trend? A serial?"

"We don't know quite yet," Mackenzie said. "We were hoping you might be able to fill in the pieces. I saw on the college website that there are only two academic advisors for the political science department, and that you're one of them. I also happen to know that both Jo Haley and Christine Lynch shared the same advisor. Would that happen to be you?"

There was a tense nervous chuckle from McMahon's end of the phone. "No. And actually, this is one of the primary reasons I have such a heavy workload right now. The other academic advisor within our department, William Holland, quit his job about three days before winter break. I got the majority of his students...and I'll likely be handling that load until they find a replacement. We have an assistant that is helping where I need it, but I've been swamped."

"Do you have any idea why Holland quit?"

"Well, there were rumblings that he had gotten involved with a student. As far as I know, there was never any evidence to support this, so I thought it was just a rumor. But when he just simply quit like that, out of nowhere, it made me wonder."

Yeah, that makes me wonder, too, Mackenzie thought.

"As far as you know, did he ever do anything else that might have been shady? Was he the type of man where news like this shocked you?"

"I can't answer with any certainty. I mean…I knew him only because we worked together. But I didn't know him much outside of work."

"So I'm going to assume you have no idea where he might live?"

"Sorry, no."

"While I have you on…Mr. McMahon, when was the last time you spoke with either Jo or Christine?"

"I never did. I was assigned them both when I was handed Holland's students, but the most I ever communicated with them was a mass email that was sent to all of the affected students." He paused here and added: "You know, given the nature of all that's happened, I could probably get Holland's address for you. I just need to make a few calls."

"I appreciate that," Mackenzie said. "But there's no need. I can get that information as well. But thank you very much for your time."

With that, she ended the call. Ellington, sitting on the edge of the bed with one shoe off and the other on, had been listening the entire time.

"Who is Holland?" he asked.

"William Holland." She filled Ellington in on all she had learned via her brief conversation with McMahon. As she did, she also sat down on the edge of the bed. She didn't realize just how tired she truly was until her feet were off of the floor.

"I'll make a call to get his information," he said. "If he works at the college, the chances are pretty good he lives around here somewhere."

"And if he *is* our guy," Mackenzie said, "my calling and leaving a message has probably freaked him out."

"Then I guess we need to act fast, then."

She nodded and realized that she had once again placed her hand on her stomach. It was almost habitual now, like someone chewing on their nails or nervously popping their knuckles.

There's life in there, she thought. *And that life, if the books are right, is feeling the same emotions I'm feeling. It's sensing my anxiousness, my happiness, my fears…*

As she listened to Ellington hunting down a physical address for William Holland, Mackenzie wondered for the first time if she had made a mistake in keeping the pregnancy from McGrath. Maybe she was taking a huge risk by remaining an active agent, out in the field.

Once this case is over, I'll tell him, she thought. *I'll focus on the baby and my mew life, and—*

Her thoughts had apparently snagged her full attention, because Ellington was looking at her now, as if waiting for a response.

"I'm sorry," she said. "I was somewhere else there for a minute."

He smiled and said, "That's okay. I got an address for one William Holland. He lives here in town, in Northwood. You feel up for a visit?"

Honestly, she didn't. The day had not been overly grueling but coming into a case directly off of a trip to Iceland and not sleeping much in the past thirty-six hours, it was all starting to catch up to her. She also knew that the growing baby inside of her was sucking some of her energy away and the thought of that actually made her smile.

Besides, even if the guy was capable of questioning or taking into custody, it probably wouldn't take that long. So she put on her best go-get-'em face and stood back up.

"Yeah, let's go pay him a visit."

Ellington stepped in front of her, making sure they were looking eye to eye. "You sure? You look tired. You even told me less than half an hour ago that you felt a little wiped out."

"It's okay. I'm good."

He kissed her on the forehead and nodded. "Okay, then. I'm going to take you on your word." With another smile, he reached down and caressed her stomach before heading for the door.

He's worried about me, she thought. *And he's already so in love with this child that it's overwhelming. He's going to be such a good father...*

But before she could latch on to that thought, they were out the door and headed for the car. They moved with such speed and purpose that it served as a reminder that she would not be able to truly focus on thoughts about their future together until this case was solved.

CHAPTER SEVEN

It was shortly after seven p.m. when Ellington parked their car in front of William Holland's house. It was a small house tucked away on the outer edges of a nice little subdivision, the sort of house that looked more like a misplaced cottage than anything else. A single car was parked in the paved driveway and several lights were on inside the house.

Ellington knocked on the door in an almost assertive way. He was not being rude about it by any means, but he was making it clear to Mackenzie that while he was worried about her health, he would be taking the lead in just about every facet of the case: driving, knocking on doors, and so on.

The door was answered by a well-groomed man who looked to be in his late forties. He wore a pair of trendy eyeglasses and was dressed in a blazer and khakis. Based on the smell wafting out of the door from behind him, he was enjoying Chinese takeout for dinner.

"William Holland?" Ellington asked.

"Yeah. And who are you?"

They both showed their badges at the same time, Mackenzie taking a single step forward as they did. "Agents White and Ellington, FBI. We understand that you left your job at Queen Nash recently."

"I did," Holland said with some uncertainty. "But I'm confused. Why would that warrant a visit from the FBI?"

"Can we come in, Mr. Holland?" Ellington asked.

Holland took a moment to think before conceding. "Sure, yeah, come on in. But I don't...I mean, what is this about?"

They entered the doorway without answering. When Holland closed the door behind them, Mackenzie took note. He'd shut it slowly and firmly. He was either nervous or scared—or, more likely, both.

"We're here in town investigating two murders," Ellington finally answered. "Both Queen Nash students, both females, and, as we've learned today, both advised by you."

They'd entered Holland's living room by then and Holland wasted no time in plopping down into a small lounge chair. He looked up to them as if he truly did not understand what they were telling him.

"Hold on…you're saying *two*?"

"Yes," Mackenzie said. "Did you not know?"

"I knew about Jo Haley. And the only reason I knew that was because we're notified by the provost whenever a student that we work with passes away. Who is the other one?"

"Christine Lynch," Mackenzie said, studying his face for a reaction. There was a flicker of recognition there, but very little. "Do you recognize the name?"

"Yes. But I…I can't recall the face. I had over sixty students, you know."

"That's another thing," Ellington said. "The *had* of it all. We hear that you quit your job shortly before winter break. Did that have anything to do with the rumors that you were seeing one of your students?"

"Ah, Jesus," Holland said. He leaned back in his chair and removed his glasses. He massaged the bridge of his nose and sighed. "Yes, I'm dating a student. I knew word was getting around and what that might do to both my career and her academic career. So I quit my job."

"Just like that?" Mackenzie asked.

"No, not *just like that*," Holland snapped. "We'd been sneaking around for months and I've fallen in love with her. She feels the same. So we talked long and hard about it, trying to figure out what to do. But during that time, it somehow became public knowledge. And that sort of made the decision for us. But…what does any of this have to do with the murders?"

"We're hoping nothing," Ellington said. "But you have to see this the way we see it. We have two murdered students and the only firm link between the two of them is that they share you as an academic advisor. Add to that the fact that you're having a fairly open relationship with a student…"

"So you think I'm a suspect? You think I killed those girls?"

Saying the words out loud seemed to make him sick. He placed his glasses back on and sat up in the chair, hunched over.

"We're not sure what we think right now," Mackenzie said. "That's why we're here to speak with you."

"Mr. Holland," Ellington said, "you just told us that you could not really place Christine Lynch's face. How about Jo Haley?"

"Yes…I knew her rather well, actually. She was a friend of the woman I'm currently seeing."

"So Jo Haley knew about the relationship?"

"I don't know. I don't think that Melissa—that's my girlfriend—would tell her. We tried our best to remain very discreet."

Mackenzie took a moment to think. The fact that his girlfriend had known one of the victims—and that the victim could have potentially known about the taboo relationship—certainly painted Holland in a worse light. It made her wonder why he would so voluntarily offer up all of this information without much of a fight.

"Forgive me for asking," Mackenzie said, "but was this girlfriend of yours—this Melissa—the first student you've ever been involved with?"

A knot of frustration worked its way across Holland's face and he got to his feet in a sudden flash of movement. "Hey, fuck you! I can't…"

"Sit back down right now," Ellington said, stepping directly into Holland's path.

Holland appeared to realize his mistake right away, his expression going from one of resigned regret to anger, back and forth as he tried to settle on an emotion.

"Look, I'm sorry. But I'm sick and tired of being judged for this and I truly don't appreciate being accused of screwing around with *all* students just because I happen to be involved in a current, responsible relationship with a consenting of-age woman."

"How old are you, Mr. Holland?" Mackenzie asked.

"Forty-five."

"And how old is Melissa?"

"Twenty-one."

"Have you ever been married?" Ellington asked, taking a step back and relaxing his posture.

"Once. For eight years. It was miserable, if you must know."

"And how did that marriage end?"

Holland shook his head and started making his way to the edge of the living room, where the foyer joined it. "Yeah, this conversation is over. Unless you plan on charging me with something, you can both get the hell out. I'm sure there are others at the college that can answer the rest of your questions."

Slowly, Mackenzie made her way to the door. Ellington followed reluctantly behind. Mackenzie turned back to him, her gut telling her there was something here.

"Mr. Holland, you understand that by failing to cooperate, it makes it look much worse for you."

"I've dealt with that for the last month or so of my life."

"Where's Melissa right now?" Ellington asked. "We'd like to speak with her as well."

"She's…" But Holland stopped here, again shaking his head. "She's been dragged through the mud, too. I won't have you bothering her over this."

"So you aren't answering any more of our questions," Ellington said. "And you're refusing to give us the location of someone else we need to speak with. Is that correct?"

"That's *absolutely* correct."

Mackenzie could tell that Ellington was getting riled up. She could see his shoulders going tense and his posture going as rigid as a stone slab. She reached out and gently touched his arm, anchoring him.

"We'll take note of that," Mackenzie said. "If we need to speak with you again in regards to this case and it's discovered that you aren't home, we'll consider you a viable suspect and you *will* be arrested. Do you understand that?"

"Sure," Holland said.

He crowded them into the foyer as he opened the door for them. The moment they were standing on the porch, Holland slammed the door.

Mackenzie started toward the porch stairs but Ellington held his ground. "You don't think it's worth pursuing?" he asked.

"Maybe. But I don't think anyone that is guilty would willingly share some of those details. Besides…we know his girlfriend's first name. If it's really pressing, we can probably weed her full name out from his records. The last thing we need, though, is the hasty arrest of an academic advisor who is already on thin ice and in a bit of controversy."

Ellington smiled and joined her heading down the stairs. "See…it's things like this that are going to make you an amazing wife. Always keeping me from doing something stupid."

"I suppose I *have* had ample practice these last few years."

They got back into the car and when Mackenzie was in the seat, she again realized how tired she was. She would never admit it to Ellington, but maybe she *did* need to take it easy.

One or two more days, little one, she thought to the growing life inside of her. *Just a few more days and you and I will be getting all the rest we want.*

CHAPTER EIGHT

She knew she shouldn't be doing this, but it was hard to resist. Besides…with a new semester on the way, this would be a good way to kick things off. One last fling. One last night of absolute craziness. And if it went the way it usually did, she'd leave feeling empowered—so empowered that it would easily override those quick little flashes of regret.

And it would be a great way to start the new semester.

Marie hadn't even tried to talk herself out of it. The moment she'd parked her car in the garage, she knew this was where she would end up tonight. All she'd had to do was make the call, to let him know that she was back in town and wanted to see him. He had never denied her before and after three weeks apart, she highly doubted he would deny her now.

And of course, he hadn't.

It was 11:05 when she walked to the back of the apartment building. It was in a sketchy part of town, but not so bad that she felt endangered by walking alone at night. Besides, it was only about eight miles away from campus and she knew that the crime rate anywhere near campus was incredibly small. Anyway, she was so excited about what the next few hours would bring that any sense of danger was long gone.

When she reached the door at the back of the building, Marie was not at all surprised that it was locked. She buzzed his apartment number and was rewarded with the sound of the lock disengaging right away. He said nothing to her through the speaker, just unlocked the door. That made her smile; he would probably be in a very serious mood. Dominant, even.

Cute, she thought. *But we know who always ends up as the aggressor…*

That thought made her even more excited as she stepped inside. She didn't even bother with the elevator, wanting to get to his apartment on the second floor as quickly as possible. She took the steps two at a time, her heart rate spiking from the exertion as well as the anticipation of what was waiting for her. The expectancy of it, from her drive down from New York to right now, approaching the apartment, was its own delicious foreplay.

It had been a long drive. She was stressed out. Tense. Man oh man, she was going to wear him out...ride him right into the ground...

When she reached his apartment, she found the door unlocked. She opened it just a crack and saw that the lights were out. Still, there was some illumination coming from the back of the main area, maybe a candle or something.

"What are you doing?" she asked, her voice sultry. She closed the door behind her and locked it.

"Waiting for you," came the answer.

"Good. But...you can't have me unless you tell me exactly what you want."

She heard him chuckle lightly somewhere in the darkness. As her eyes adjusted to the lack of light, she could see his shape in the living room, lying on the couch. She smiled and started to walk over to him.

The apartment smelled dusty and unused—mainly because that's exactly what it was. She knew he had a better place, but she also knew that he did not like to have her there. He liked to keep his personal life private. From what she understood about him, he spent very little time at home. She'd only seen the outside of it, usually meeting with him here or, on a few occasions, the back seat of his car or a hotel. While she understood the need for privacy, she also wished she could just ravage him in a huge bed for once, maybe with some mood lighting and music.

But keeping it all hidden was sexy, too. It was part of the allure. It was why she was practically fighting back to the urge to pounce on him right then and there.

But their trysts had always been about the build-up. Teasing, some rough foreplay, even some playfully derogatory remarks from time to time.

"Come to me, Marie," he said.

She did, approaching the couch and finding him still fully dressed. That was fine with her; it would just stretch the foreplay out for longer.

"That's cute," she said as she knelt on the floor in front of him. She kissed him softly, flicking her tongue against his lips in a way she knew he liked.

"What's cute?" he asked.

"You, thinking you're in control here."

"Oh, I am," he said, sitting up.

"I'll let you think that for a while," she said, nibbling at the soft flesh of his neck. He stirred against it and she felt his hands on her—one at her back, another at the back of her head. "But we both know the tr—"

Without warning, he grabbed her by the back of the head and jammed her head forward. She was pushed forward with violent speed, her forehead slamming into his knee.

"What the…"

But before she could get the question out, he was on top of her, pressing his full weight into her back. Her head reeled from the strike and for a moment, Marie legitimately had no idea where she was.

As she got her hands under her to fight back against him, his hands were in her long blonde hair again. This time, he drove her head hard into the wood floor. Marie fought against it for a moment, but she quickly started to feel the world swimming away as a flaring pain radiated in the back of her head.

Somewhere very far away, she was aware of him grabbing her by the waist of her pants and pulling them down. Then the world went black for a moment and she only came to after that because she felt his mouth on her, roaming seemingly everywhere.

It made no sense. She would let him do just about anything to her and would, in return, do just about anything for him. So why would he…?

This thought was also interrupted by the floating darkness that came and went. But this time when it came, it stayed for quite a while.

***

It had involved more work than he'd thought but he was finally able to relax around two in the morning. The hardest part of all had been knocking her unconscious. He simply didn't think he'd have it in him. Strangling people was one thing. It was just a matter of convincing yourself to do it and then applying the pressure once their neck was in his hands. But slamming Marie's head into the floor had taken more grit than he had been expecting.

When she was out, the rest of the work was hard but enjoyable. And as he went about the tasks, he started to feel comfortable with the decision he had made.

He'd killed Jo Haley and Christine Lynch outright. With Jo, he'd slept with her, enjoyed the encounter immensely, and then strangled her when round two had gotten started. And perhaps the sex was to blame, but he had almost changed his mind—had almost chickened out. He'd learned a lesson there and opted to skip the sex when it had come to Christine. And then her body had been found and he'd seen the story on the news—just a blip, really, but an eye-opener all the same. It had made him rethink things…that he couldn't *just* kill them.

But he had to retain them. The ones beyond Christine, the ones that needed to be silenced. There would be more, including Marie. And if he could not kill them outright and just leave them where they fell, that meant he had to do something else. He had to be more discreet, more careful.

He looked at his work and thought he would be fully capable of getting away with it. He stood in front of the opened coat closet that was located in the hallway. Marie was in the closet, completely nude and hanging by her bound wrists from the coat rack that ran horizontal across the width of the closet. There were also three strips of reinforced duct tape covering her mouth. Her body was hanging downward but her arms were stretched up over her head from where he had tied her wrists together. It was an oddly seductive pose and it made him regret not sleeping with her before he'd taken her captive.

He'd been standing there, staring at her and enjoying the sense of power and accomplishment, for nearly fifteen minutes before Marie started to stir. She let out a little groan, trying to lean forward and sleepily realizing that she was being held in place. This seemed to alert her, her eyes flaring open and her legs standing upright. She looked around feverishly, taking in her situation: aching head, stark naked, bound to an iron bar in a coat closet, being watched with malicious intent by a man she had been sleeping with quite regularly over the past two months.

She tried to speak, a single syllable trapped by the duct tape. A sound that he thought as a question: "What?"

It was the only word she could get out as the severity of the situation came slamming into her.

He walked up to her and cupped her chin in his right hand. She jerked back away from him only to find that it caused her bound arms to pull back at an awkward angle. He slowly ran his hand down from her chin, across her right breast, toward her inner thighs. For the first time since they had started sleeping together, she closed her legs to him as he explored downward.

He laughed at her. In return, she tried screaming through the tape. It sounded like someone might be running a vacuum cleaner elsewhere in the apartment. He had shut her mouth off well, stretching the tape from ear to ear, reinforced three times.

"No need for that," he said. He did his best to ignore his flesh-driven needs and the excitement that pinged every nerve in his body. There were important things to get down to here—things to discuss and sort out.

She moaned in response, silenced by the tape.

"There are some things you and I need to talk about," he said. He then showed her the gun he had been hiding behind his back—a gun he had picked up two years ago and had never used. He'd only ever picked it up a single time since purchasing it. And he honestly had no intention of using it now.

Of course, there was no way Marie knew that.

"If you scream or try to call out for help, I'll kill you." He walked forward again, pressing the side of his face to hers. He placed his free hand on her hip and pulled her forward. He then pushed the barrel of the gun into her bare stomach. "Do you believe me?"

She nodded frantically. There was hurt and severe confusion in her eyes as the tears started to come.

For a moment, he wondered if the gun would be preferable. It would certainly be over quicker.

No...it would be too loud. And I'd miss out on that exquisite moment the light goes out of her eyes.

He leaned back against the wall again, brandishing the gun as if it were nothing more than a cup of coffee.

And then he began to talk. He talked and he accused, and he did his very best to keep from strangling her right then and there. Even when he ripped the tape from her face and allowed her to speak in little trembling whispers, he managed not to kill her.

But the answers he got from her and the way she responded to him...he was pretty sure he would be strangling her soon. For a moment, as he had been tying her up, he convinced himself that if she gave him all of the information he wanted, he might release her.

But that was ridiculous. She'd never be able to *not* turn him in—to report what he had done to her.

So she was going to have to die, too. Like the other two.

As this thought dawned on him, he found himself pleased to find that with each murder he committed, the concept got easier and easier to accept.

CHAPTER NINE

Back at the hotel, Mackenzie wrapped up her day with a hot bath. She typically wasn't a fan of taking baths in hotel rooms but her feet and calves were aching, and her mind was reeling. She just wanted to relax. Had she not been sixteen weeks pregnant, she would have likely enjoyed a few glasses of wine as well.

She replayed the visit to William Holland's home over and over in her head. Her instincts told her that he likely had no role in the murders—that he just happened to have quite a few coincidences stacked against him. She also knew that the fact he had been so insistent on not providing information about his girlfriend might only mean that he was regretting the sacrifices he was having to make in order to make the relationship work. Giving up a fairly prestigious job just so he could have regular sex with a younger woman seemed like one hell of a sacrifice, even if he *was* falling in love with her.

Despite all of that, she thought it might be worth the trouble of trying to get in touch with Holland's current girlfriend. Even if Holland was a dead end, maybe she would also know Jo and Christine. Maybe she'd have some information on them that could—

Her attention was broken by a knock at the bathroom door. It cracked open and Ellington peeked inside. "Am I okay to come in?"

"Sure."

He gave her a playful *whoa* look as he stepped into the bathroom. She enjoyed the way he looked at her when she was naked. It wasn't necessarily a lustful sort of leering, but one of appreciation. Even now, when the beginning of her baby belly was beginning to announce itself, she could see it in his eyes.

"You're going to look sexy as hell with a baby belly," he said. He removed her towel from the lowered toilet seat and sat down. His eyes still roamed her body through the steam of the hot water.

"I heard you on the phone," Mackenzie said. "Anything new?"

"No. I just put in a request for any records on William Holland. I was going to start down a trail to try to find whatever Melissa he might be dating but that's going to be incredibly hard without college resources."

"You really think he's an avenue worth pursuing?" she asked.

"Honestly…no. Someone that gives up on keeping his relationship with a student a secret so easily would make a lousy killer. Plus, he didn't seem like he was trying to hide any information. He was giving it freely."

Mackenzie nodded. She checked her fingers and found them pruny. She wrinkled her nose at this and then gestured for her towel. Ellington handed it to her and she stood up to dry off. As she did, she looked down at her stomach skeptically.

"Did you mean what you said?" she asked. "About me getting a baby belly?"

"I did. Of course, I've never been with a woman with a baby belly. I'm just making a general assumption."

"You know, I've noticed my fingers starting to swell."

Ellington seemed unsure what to say about this. He took her in his arms after she wrapped the towel around her and kissed her forehead.

"My ankles are swelling, too," she said. "All of it is coming so fast. I know it's incredibly vain, but I'm concerned what this baby is going to do to my body."

"You mean health-wise or appearance wise?" he asked.

"Both."

"I hate to break it to you," Ellington said. "But you and I…we're married now. The only man that *better* be looking at you is me. And I can tell you with a great deal of certainty that when that baby belly comes and your ankles are all swollen and you're waddling around like a duck…I'm still going to find you sexy."

She laughed softly against his chest and hugged him. "Waddling?"

"I wasn't sure what word to use. Sorry."

"It's okay. It was cute."

She kissed him softly and took his hands. "I'm beyond exhausted. But I think if you get creative, you can maybe find a way for me to stay awake for a while longer. If you want."

Ellington's only response was finding the overlap of the towel at her back and pulling it undone. As it fell to the floor, he picked her up and carried her into the bedroom where, as Mackenzie had suggested, he did indeed keep her awake for a good while longer.

***

Perhaps it was finally solving her father's murder roughly a year ago, but her nightmares and dreams had stopped featuring those rustic old cornfields that had haunted her back in Nebraska. Now, whenever her mind slipped into a dream, it was less vivid and almost fluid in a way. She had always had incredibly vivid dreams and the ones she could remember were as clear as the memories of movies or TV shows in her head.

Sometime after she fell asleep after being utterly satisfied by Ellington, Mackenzie dreamt that she was standing in a large room. The room was the size of a concert hall and only contained two pieces of furniture: a rocking chair and a bassinet. The sound of a baby crying was coming from the bassinet, echoing through the enormous room so that it nearly sounded like thunder.

Mackenzie ran across the room but she never seemed to get any closer to the bassinet. The baby continued to cry, now escalating into high-pitched screams. She had not been around many babies in her time but she could tell the difference between cries meaning that the baby needed to be changed or was hungry and cries of terror.

She finally reached the bassinet, gasping and out of breath. When she looked inside, there was no baby. Instead, the entire inside was covered in blood. She reached in to touch it and found it still wet and warm. She then raised the blood to her face, examining it closely, as if she had never seen it before. And as she did, the blood ran down her fingers, dribbling over the new shiny wedding band on her ring finger.

"Mac?"

She turned around and saw Ellington. He was holding a baby. It did not appear to be moving and it was most certainly not crying. "What happened?" Ellington asked. "Oh my God, Mac, what happened?"

Mackenzie ran toward him, screaming now. And when she reached him, she looked to the baby and saw—

She sat up in bed with a little cry.

Ellington still slept soundly beside her and the hotel room was mostly quiet with the exception of the humming heater against the wall. She gazed at the bedside clock and saw that it was 3:55. She'd fallen asleep shortly after ten, giving her about six hours of sleep. She was sure that wasn't enough to be fully recharged but she also knew that finding sleep after that doozy of a nightmare was going to be next to impossible.

She felt her stomach, as if assuring herself it *had* just been a dream. She knew that it was far too early in the pregnancy, but she found herself wishing that the baby would kick or stir some way.

To get her mind off of the panic and worry the dream had caused, Mackenzie focused on the current case. William Holland had left a bad taste in her mouth, and even though she felt confident he was not at all involved in the murders, something about him seemed to point to something else—some clue or lead that she could not quite identify. Perhaps speaking to his girlfriend would help in that regard.

She then thought of the victims, going through a little comparison chart in her head. Her eyes were closed, trying to both sort through her thoughts and fall asleep all at once. She listened to the hum of the heater, focused on her breathing, and zoned out in a lazy sort of meditation.

Both women were strangled. The killer slept with Jo before strangling her. Why not Christine? What changed? There was no sign of actual penetration, but there was physical evidence on her underwear that she had been at the very least in a state of arousal upon her death. So they are linked but there are also differences.

The victims were sexually attracted to this man. Maybe he was even using sex as a lure for them. That's why they allowed him in. These are planned murders. And maybe murders of passion...or simple control.

Intercourse with the first victim and not the second indicates that perhaps he found the act of sex a waste of time...or unnecessary. Therefore, maybe it's not entirely power and control he wants. Not having sex with Christine could mean that he learned some lessons that first time with Jo. Maybe he's being quicker...more careful. Maybe he only wants the deaths now...not the lead up to it.

She pondered all of this and was surprised to feel sleep sneaking back up on her. She was fine with that. Her little thinking session had pointed her toward a few solid assumptions about their killer.

He's being invited in by these women; they are openly welcoming him before he kills them. He's also new to murder. He's learning as he goes, finding out what he is capable of and what he enjoys—what he has time for and what is too time consuming. And if he's still learning and feels as if he's in a hurry when he's in the act, he's bound to make a mistake sooner rather than later. He's likely already made one...we just need to find out what it is.

That was the final thought on her mind as she drifted off back to sleep. It was enough to make her feel confident about the next day or so. But she also knew that with a slew of students returning to campus the following day, she and Ellington would have their work cut out for them.

CHAPTER TEN

At eight o' clock the following morning, Mackenzie and Ellington were sitting on a bench in the hallway of Queen Nash's political science department. There was a closed door directly to their right, a black placard just beneath the tinted glass that read CHARLES McMAHON. Mackenzie had made a call earlier, setting up a meeting with McMahon as early as possible. While she had done that, Ellington had been speaking on the phone with Agent Yardley back in DC, finding out that William Holland had a squeaky clean record.

Ellington sipped from a cup of coffee they had picked up at a nearby shop on the way to campus. He grimaced and sighed. "This would taste so much better if we were sitting by a dying campfire in Iceland."

Mackenzie didn't have the heart to tell him that the coffee he had prepared by that beloved campfire had tasted like burnt coffee beans, so she only nodded and sipped from her own cup.

A few seconds later, a man came walking quickly in their direction. Students had been walking up and down the halls all morning, but this was the first person they had seen who was clearly a member of the faculty. He gave them both a nod and a smile as he approached the door, digging in the side pocket of a laptop bag that was slung over his shoulder. This, apparently, was Charles McMahon.

"Sorry," he said, pulling a set of keys out of the pocket of the laptop bag. "The first day back after winter break is always a little rushed. And then I got your call and that just added to it all…"

"It's okay," Mackenzie said. "We appreciate you meeting with us on such short notice."

Still flustered, McMahon unlocked his door and stepped inside. "Come on in," he said.

As Mackenzie and Ellington took the pair of seats in front of his desk, McMahon set about getting things in order. As he did so, he spoke to them as best he could. After he slid his laptop out of the bag and up onto his desk, he did his best to give them his undivided attention.

"On the phone, you said you might need my help again," he said. "What can I do for you?"

"Well," Mackenzie said, "we spoke to William Holland. He admitted that he is indeed having a relationship with a student and it *is* why he quit his job. We asked for his girlfriend's information and he was very defensive."

"He seemed to forget that we work for the FBI," Ellington remarked. "And that we can get the information other ways. We were hoping that *other way* would be you."

"I'll do my best. What information do you need?"

"All we know is the woman's first name. Melissa. We were hoping you could help us figure out who that is. We assume she was once a student that was using Holland as an advisor."

"That would be a safe bet," McMahon said. "I do know that the relationship is fairly recent. Based on the gossip, anyway."

"No more than a year based on what Holland told us," Ellington said. "Is there any way you can look back over his records for names of students to find a name for us?"

"The best I can do is go over the list of students that were transferred to me after Holland quit. If you need anything more than that, you'll have to go way over my head. Give me one second and I can look through the names."

Mackenzie and Ellington waited patiently as McMahon stopped in mid-setup to log into his computer and find the information. He worked quickly, humming under his breath as he did so. Mackenzie thought he had a slight edge of irritation to him, his holiday break no doubt hampered by the fact that he had a much larger workload thanks to Holland and his extracurricular activities.

After about two minutes of searching, McMahon started to jot down something on a nearby notepad. "I've got two Melissas that came to me from Holland's group," he said. "One is a freshman and the other is a junior."

"Holland said his girlfriend is twenty-one," Mackenzie said. "Is it safe to assume, then, that it's not the freshman?"

"Yeah, that's a very safe bet." McMahon slid the sheet of notepad paper he had been scribbling on over to them. "Her name is Melissa Evington. This is the phone number I have on file for her."

Mackenzie took it and placed it in her pocket. "Can you recall ever meeting with her before the winter break?"

"Honestly, I don't. I can look back through my schedule to make sure, but I saw so many kids because of what got dumped on me from Holland…"

"That's quite all right," Ellington said. "The name and the number are more than enough."

"Good," said McMahon. "Hopefully she'll be of some help." He paused here and then added: "Agents…is this something that we need to alert the students about? I know these murders didn't happen on campus, but still…"

"It's a little too early to make any sort of formal announcement," Mackenzie said. "But the local PD will ultimately make that decision."

McMahon nodded, but slowly, as if he wasn't the biggest fan of that answer. And honestly, Mackenzie understood. Women were being killed by a man they apparently trusted; she felt that the student population *should* know about it sooner rather than later. But if panic could be avoided, she was all for that as well.

Yet another reason to wrap this thing as quickly as possible, she thought as she and Ellington left the office of Charles McMahon.

***

They managed to catch Melissa Evington later in the day in between classes and appointments. Mackenzie had called the number McMahon had given her and squared things away. From that brief conversation, Mackenzie felt as if they might be walking into a lost cause.

When they met her in a little café within the student commons, Melissa Evington looked pissed off. When she spotted Mackenzie and Ellington sitting together, she walked toward them and seemed to go out of her way to let them know she was being inconvenienced.

As Melissa came over to them, Mackenzie wondered why she would be messing around with a man nearly twenty-five years older than her. She was absolutely gorgeous, even through her over-acted anger. She was the kind of young woman who had the looks to make women like Mackenzie—not quite ten years older than her—long for her youth, wondering what opportunities she might have missed.

"I hate to be a bitch," Melissa said, "but I can give you maybe ten minutes. I've got to meet with a peer group in half an hour to nail down an assignment."

"If you answer our questions without any reservations," Ellington said, "ten minutes should be plenty."

"You said it was about my relationship with William," she said. "I assure you, it's a consenting relationship. And no, I'm not with him for a good grade, as some people seem to think."

"We've spoken with him, too," Mackenzie said. "And based on what he said, it does seem to be a solid relationship. What we need to ask you, though, is if you know whether or not he's done this before."

"This? You mean dating a student?"

Mackenzie nodded.

"No. He hasn't. He was married, then got divorced. I'm not quite sure how much time passed between the divorce being finalized and he and I dating."

"Do you know why he and his wife divorced?" Ellington asked.

"She wanted kids and he didn't."

"You know that for certain?" Mackenzie asked.

"It's what he told me. Look…what do you think he's doing?"

Mackenzie leaned forward and lowered her voice. "Two students have been murdered in the span of the last ten days. They both seemed to have been killed by men they knew well. Well enough to engage in sexual activities with them. The kicker here is that both women were being advised by William Holland."

Melissa looked as if someone had slapped her hard across the face. "And that makes him a suspect?"

"Well, it seems coincidental. But then when you add in the fact that he's currently dating a twenty-one-year-old—right around the same age as the other women—yes, it sort of makes him worth looking into."

Melissa's anger slid back toward irritation and then the reality of what Mackenzie had said dawned on her. "Two students? Can you tell me their names?"

"Jo Haley and Christine Lynch."

Melissa sat back hard in her chair. Some of the color went right out of her face. "Christine? You're sure?"

"Yes. You knew her, I take it?"

"I did. She was in two of my classes last semester."

"Do you know anything about her or her circle of friends?" Ellington asked.

"No. I just know she was dating some guy that lives around here. I think she was also from somewhere out in California. But I…Jesus, I don't believe it."

"What about Jo Haley?" Mackenzie asked. "Did you know her?"

"No, I don't recognize the name."

Mackenzie was about to follow up with another question but her phone rang instead. She answered it and turned away from the table for privacy.

"This is Agent White."

"Agent White, this is Deputy Wheeler. I thought you and your partner might want to know that someone came forward this morning...said they live in the same building Christine Lynch lived in. She's got some details from that night I think you might want to hear."

"Who's the witness? You got a number or address?"

"Oh, she's still right here at the precinct. I asked if she'd be willing to wait to speak to you."

"Give us half an hour. Thanks, Wheeler."

She ended the call and turned back to Melissa. Ellington was still speaking with her so she let him run the course. "Do you remember Mr. Holland ever speaking about either Jo or Christine? Even something just in passing?"

"No. Or, if he did, I just didn't really pay much attention to it."

Mackenzie reached under the table and gave Ellington's knee a little squeeze, a sign that it was time to wrap the conversation.

"Well, we know you're very busy on this first day back from break," Mackenzie said. "So we'll let you get back to it. Thank you for your time."

"Sure...sure," Melissa said, still clearly rocked by the news of the two murders. She got up and left the table, taking one look back as if she didn't quite trust the agents.

"Who was the call from?" Ellington asked.

"Deputy Wheeler," she said, getting to her feet. "We've got a witness from the night Christine Lynch was killed."

"Who?"

"Don't know," she said as they stood up to leave.

Mackenzie took two steps before she felt a quick wash of fatigue sweep over her. For a split second, she felt incredibly dizzy and there was a slight feeling of vertigo that seemed to pass all the way through her body.

She paused, holding herself against a nearby table. *You've got to remember that you're pregnant,* she told herself. *You're investigating for two now.*

"Mac? You okay?" Ellington was at her side at once, clearly concerned.

"Yeah."

"I love you...but don't bullshit me."

48

"I'm fine. I just stood up too fast and got disoriented."

"Would it have happened if there wasn't a human being growing inside of you?" he asked with a snarky tone.

"Probably not."

He eyed her with caution and took her hand. "Please take it easy. If I have to pull the protective husband card, I will. But I don't want to argue…so if you start to feel sick, please tell me."

"I will. But I'm fine right now. I swear it."

He gave her a hesitant nod and then, still hand in hand, they left the café and headed back out into the afternoon where a potentially huge lead was waiting for them.

CHAPTER ELEVEN

Things were a little tense on the drive to the precinct. Mackenzie did not like the feeling that Ellington was being overprotective of her, especially not in the middle of a case. She understood it and even appreciated it but she was already seeing where his role as a husband was going to be a bit more domineering and harder to navigate than his role as a partner. It was apparently a sensation he was feeling, too. The ride to the precinct was absent of any conversation as they both sifted through their thoughts in their own way.

When they arrived at the precinct, Deputy Wheeler was waiting for them. He looked very much on edge as he led them to the back of the building. He gave a few nods to his fellow officers here and there but seemed otherwise intensely focused on the task at hand. Mackenzie decided she liked him quite a bit—a cop who took his job seriously and approached it with a sense of pride.

He led them to a small conference room where an older woman sat at a table. She was sipping from a cup of tea when they entered. Mackenzie thought she might be of Filipino descent from the shade of her skin. She looked a little nervous, almost like she regretted even coming forward with her information.

"Agents," Wheeler said, "this is Hazel Isidro. She came forward with some information you might find helpful in the Christine Lynch case."

With that said, Wheeler seemed unsure if he should stay or so. He opted to simply stand by the door while Mackenzie and Ellington took seats at the small table.

"I understand you live in the same building as Christin Lynch did," Mackenzie said.

"That's right," Hazel said. "She was on the third floor. I live on the second."

"Did you know her well?"

"Not *well*. But she was a very friendly young lady. On two different occasions over the past half a year or so, she happened to be coming into the building the same time as me after I had gone grocery shopping. She insisted on helping me with my bags. A very friendly young lady for sure. But we did not speak much, no."

"Did you ever see her with a man?" Ellington asked.

"I saw her leaving with a young man a few times. Two or three times, maybe. She never introduced him."

"Do you recall what he looked like?"

"Not really. Just brown hair, close cut. A handsome young man for sure."

"Young, as in Christine's age?" Mackenzie asked.

"I'd say so, yes."

Mackenzie and Ellington shared a look and had one of those nearly telepathic moments good partners (and, she had heard, husbands and wives) often shared. *Probably Clark Manners,* they both seemed to think toward one another.

"Okay, so share with us the information you came to the precinct with today," Mackenzie said.

"Well, it was three nights ago. I'd been suffering with this awful toothache all day. Took some Motrin for it but it barely touched it. I went to sleep and woke up around one in the morning with it hurting like crazy. I was in tears from the pain. So I walked out to the Walgreens two blocks down from the apartment building and got some high-strength stuff. On the way back, I opened the door and when I did, this man approached me from behind. Asked me to hold the door. Usually, at such an hour, I probably would have thought it was sort of sketchy and not held the door. But I was just in so much pain and wanted to get back to bed…I didn't even think twice about it."

"Did you get a good look at him?" Ellington asked.

"No. He was wearing this black hoodie…most of his head was covered. It was one of those moments that, even though I was in pain, I realized how stupid it was for me to let him in and…"

She stopped here and looked up at them with sorrow in her eyes. A thought was coming to her, dawning on her as if the thought had not crossed her mind until that very moment.

"My God…is it my fault? Did I let the killer in? Is it my fault she'd dead?"

"It's far too early to even begin making such claims," Mackenzie said. "We don't even know that this man you let in was the man that killed Christine."

Hazel nodded, but it was obvious that she seemed uncertain. Slowly, she went on. "I took the elevator up mainly because I was tired and in pain and just…out of it, you know? But this man went right for the stairs. He moved quickly, sort of like he was in a hurry. When he passed by the elevator, that's when I got the best look at him. Just a bit of his face, from around the side of the hood."

"Any guess as to what his age might be?" Ellington asked.

"No, sorry."

"Any chance it might have been the young man you'd seen Christine with?" Mackenzie asked.

"No, I don't think so. This man was much taller. Easily half a foot taller than I am. Maybe a little over six feet tall."

"Can you be as accurate as possible about the timeframe of all of this?"

"Well, it was sometime after twelve thirty when I woke up; I don't remember the exact time. But I clearly remember that it was one ten when I settled back into bed because I did the sleep-math to see how much sleep I'd end up getting. So it was probably right around twelve forty when I let that man into the building."

Mackenzie turned back to Wheeler. "Can you get your guys to go back through the video footage to look for Ms. Isidro and this man in the black hoodie?"

"Absolutely," Wheeler said, taking his leave right away.

"Can I ask, why did you wait so long to come forward with this?" Ellington asked.

"Well, I honestly didn't even think about it again. I ended up going to the dentist the following day and it just sort of went out of my mind. But then this morning, one of my neighbors told me about Christine and it came roaring back. That's when I realized just how shady that man seemed…and how I really sort of screwed up by letting him in."

"Again," Mackenzie said, "we can't automatically assume the two things are related." *Though based on the timeline,* she thought, *there might be a very good chance they are.*

"Does this neighbor maybe know more about Christine than you did?" Mackenzie asked.

"I don't think so. She—"

She was interrupted as the door to the conference room came flying open. Wheeler leaned in—the front half of his body leaning in and everything from the stomach down still out. He looked a little excited, a little scared.

"Sorry, agents," he said, the excitement also clear in his voice. "But we just got a dispatch call from a unit that's out on patrol. We found   another   body."

CHAPTER TWELVE

The body had been discovered along the banks of the Patapsco River, on a dry bank about twenty-five minutes away from campus. When Mackenzie and Ellington arrived with Deputy Wheeler in tow, the original two policemen who had discovered the body were still there. Their patrol car was parked on the side of the road inconspicuously, hiding the sight of the river that flowed below a small decline beyond the ditch at the side of the road. Fortunately, it was a secondary road and the traffic wasn't too bad.

Mackenzie barely stopped to speak to the officers as she made her way to the ditch and the wooded area beyond. "Who discovered the body?" she asked.

"A Department of Transportation crew," one of the officers said. "They were out here to remove a deer that had been hit on the side of the road, about thirty feet down that way," he said, nodding to the left. "Said he just happened to see something weird sticking up out of the water out there."

"Is the scene untouched?" she asked.

"Yeah. We only saw the body and called it in. Haven't touched a single thing."

Mackenzie and Ellington made their way into the thin strip of woodland that separated the secondary road from the bank of the Patapsco. Wheeler elected to stay behind with his fellow officers.

Even before they made it into the tree line, she could see the outline of what was clearly a human leg, sticking out of the water and partially grounded along the bank. She found it easily believable that anyone driving at a slow speed—just like a Department of Transportation vehicle having just picked up a deer carcass—would be able to see it if they happened to be looking out of their window.

They came to the bank and more of the body came into view. As they neared the water, all of the details came into focus. The victim was a young woman—probably somewhere between eighteen and twenty-four. She had been stripped completely naked. There were faint streaks of red in her blonde hair, likely blood. There were small scrapes and cuts along most of her body. The most prominent feature, though, was that her right arm had clearly

53

been broken. It was bent back at an angle, raised over her head where it was bound to her left wrist.

"Well, the age range certainly fits," Ellington said.

Mackenzie nodded as she went to her haunches to get a better look. The woman's body was mostly on its back, but tilted up just enough by the bank and a stray log that had caught her body and, likely, had been the cause of her being mired in this location. The parts of the woman's back and buttocks that Mackenzie could see were very scratched up. A few areas looked as if someone had taken a sheet of sandpaper to her flesh. Most of those nicks and scratches were still bleeding.

"She hasn't been dead long," she commented. "Sure, she's pale, but that's because she's been exposed to water that's barely above freezing. But a lot of these wounds are still bleeding."

"You think this was just a killer being lazy in disposing of the body or what?"

"No. The abrasions on her back seem to mostly be going in the same direction. I think she was dumped elsewhere and the river carried her here."

"So she was dumped somewhere from up that way," Ellington said, pointing in the direction the river was lazily drifting from.

"It feels...*off*. The others were strangled and left where they were. Being dumped in a river is a huge leap from that."

"I'll give you that," Ellington said. "But we have to consider the age. And while I hate to say it about a dead woman, she's what most would consider attractive—like the other two."

"We need to ID her," Mackenzie said. "And if we start by secluding the search to only Queen Nash students, we'll know if this body is linked to Jo Haley and Christine Lynch pretty quickly."

"I don't see evidence of strangulation," Ellington said. "You?"

"No." But still, something about the way the body had been discarded made her go back to a particular train of thought she'd entertained while trying to get back to sleep from her nightmare.

Jo Haley's death seemed to have been thought out. The killer had sex with her, then strangled her. Then with Christine, he was more cautious, more direct. While there might have been *some* sexual activity between them, they did not have intercourse and she was simply strangled.

Maybe with this one, he was trying to be even more careful. Perhaps that's why she's been bound. Or maybe he found himself in a bigger hurry. Maybe he's even starting to realize how similar his murders seem and is trying to vary things...

"Your gut is usually right," Ellington said. "As your *husband*, that's difficult to say. But it's true. What's it say about this?"

She didn't hesitate much before she answered: "I think if we start with just searching Queen Nash records, we'll have an ID on this girl by nightfall. I also think if she was assigned William Holland as an advisor, he's going to see the inside of an interrogation room very soon."

As if summoned by the urgency of the situation and Mackenzie's comment, Wheeler came walking through the brush. He seemed to take great pains to not look at the body. "Thought you might want to know that Forensics is on the way. They're about ten minutes out."

Mackenzie only nodded. She looked back down to the body—a beautiful female in the prime of her life. Someone's daughter. Someone's daughter with a future that would never be fully realized.

Habitually, Mackenzie's hand once again found the minuscule bulge in her stomach and remained there, as if protecting what was inside.

CHAPTER THIRTEEN

Mackenzie and Ellington were working in one of the precinct's smaller conference rooms when a positive ID of the victim from the river came in. It was 6:27 and, working under Mackenzie's guidance of narrowing the fingerprint and facial recognition search to Queen Nash University students, it had been a much easier process than it might have been.

Wheeler entered the room with a printout and happily slid it across the table to them. "Positive ID," he said.

Mackenzie picked up the paper and read some of the highlights out loud. As she did, a stirring of excitement started to come alive in her stomach. *That,* she thought with a trace of irony, *or the baby senses your excitement.*

"Marie Totino, twenty years of age. Currently enrolled at Queen Nash in her junior year. Political science major. She's done some interning in DC and with the state government for Maryland. Lives in Baltimore, close to campus. Originally from Bethesda."

"Any word on her academic advisor?" Ellington asked.

"It's listed as Charles McMahon."

"Also," Wheeler reported, "Forensics did find some harsh marks around the base of her neck. Might be evidence of strangulation. We'll know for sure after the autopsy, I'd guess. There was also a large bruise on her head and a small fracture in the skull within that area. They also found residue around her mouth that indicates her mouth had been taped shut at some point."

"Any idea when she was last seen?" Mackenzie asked.

"We've got a few guys working on that right now. The family is being notified as we speak. Marie was an only child. Both parents still alive, living in Bethesda. There could be more, but I literally got all of this information just as that sheet came in."

Mackenzie and Ellington got to their feet, starting to work in a kind of sync that felt natural yet, at the same time, almost *super*natural in a way. They were going to have to speak with the family. Mackenzie hated speaking with aggrieved loved ones so close to getting the traumatic news of the passing of someone they cared about, but timing was everything on this case. With a third body discovered and now identified as another student, there was no way to keep the story contained—especially now that classes had resumed.

"Where are you on finding anything relevant on the security footage from Christine Lynch's apartment building?"

"Nothing of use. We have the guy coming in from the front and the western side, but his face is never shown. We even have the moment where he and Hazel Isidro cross paths, but there's only the slightest bit of his face. The tip of a nose and just a flash of brow. Nothing we can use to ID."

"I'd like to see that footage when we get back," Mackenzie said. "For now, though, we're going to need the home address of Marie Totino's family."

"Sure," Wheeler said. "I'll get that for you right now."

Wheeler left them and the moment the door closed, Ellington took Mackenzie's hand. "Remember when I threatened to play my protective husband card?"

"I do. It was funny."

"I'm being serious," he said. "Mac, do you really think it's the best idea for you to be speaking to a woman that just lost her daughter? If you think I haven't noticed your hand going to your belly whenever something stressful comes up, you're blind."

His care for her was heartwarming but she also felt like he was maybe being a little *too* overprotective. She honestly didn't think it was worth an argument, though. "Fine," she said. "You take the lead when we get there then."

He looked at her for a moment and she was pretty certain she could read the thought behind his eyes. *He thinks I should have stayed at home on this one. He thinks it was a mistake not to tell McGrath about my pregnancy.*

Maybe he was right. But they were too deep into this now, so there was no sense in dwelling on it.

"Let's just try to wrap this thing as quickly as we can," Ellington said. "Then we won't have to worry about these things."

"With that sort of in-depth thinking, you should *definitely* be leading," she said with a thin smile.

"Oh my God, I hope our kid doesn't get your smart-ass streak."

With that, they left the conference room in search of Wheeler and the address of a family that had just lost their daughter to what appeared to be a serial killer.

***

True to her word, Mackenzie let Ellington take the lead when they arrived at the Totino house thirty-five minutes later. And honestly, she was glad he was taking the lead role. The parents—fifty-two-year-old Sandra Totino and fifty-seven year old Mike Totino—were a little less than an hour into their new lives without a child. The news was so fresh that the police who had visited to break the news were just making their way back to their patrol car as Mackenzie and Ellington arrived.

Now, fifteen minutes later, they were sitting in the Totinos' living room. Sandra looked to be in a daze, rocking back and forth from her place the couch and looking to the floor. It was Mike, the father, who did all of the talking. Mackenzie was pretty sure the only thing that was allowing him to have any sort of rational conversation with them was his anger—at a killer that had taken his daughter…at a killer he wanted very badly to be caught and brought to justice as quickly as possible.

"Your daughter makes the third female student that has been killed in less than two weeks," Ellington said once the Totinos had managed to get some semblance of emotional order to themselves. It was clear they both had a long way to go (and understandably so) but Mike was hanging on by sheer anger alone.

"Why in God's name would someone target Marie, though?" Mike Totino asked.

"That's exactly what we're hoping you can help us with. We believe that all of the victims had some sort of relationship with the killer—be it a simple friendship or something more intimate."

"I don't believe Marie had a boyfriend," Mike said. He then added, with a bit of venom in his voice: "If that's what you're insinuating."

Ellington let the jab slide right by, unaffected. "We believe that if we can find just one link between the victims, it might help us get that much closer to identifying the killer. Do you know any of Marie's close friends?"

"That's what makes this so hard. I wouldn't go so far as to say that Marie doesn't have…*didn't have*…any friends…" He stopped here, clearly gulping down a sob. It took him several seconds to get composure before he continued on again. "These last several months, she hung out with this political group. They put on these rallies and fundraisers, you know? She mentioned a few names here and there, but I never paid much attention to the names. How about you, dear?"

He nudged Sandra but she could only manage a slow shake of the head. Tears were still flowing down her cheeks but her face was a blank slate.

"Her records show that she was very involved in politics," Ellington said. "She had a few internships for government bodies, right?"

"She did," Mike said.

"Do you remember what the internships were for?"

"The most recent one was something to help promote voter registration. But there was some other one she was involved in...helping a campaign manager with schedules and things like that."

"And she never mentioned any of the people she was working with?"

"No. She was never one to really care about her social life. She was always more interested in making a career out of it. She has been since she was about sixteen. She always been very politically minded. She knew that neither of us," he said, pointing to himself and then to his wife, "cared much for politics. But Marie tried pushing it on us. Bringing us fliers and pamphlets. Pins and flags and all this other stuff for candidates she believed in."

He had another moment here, choked up by the memory of his daughter's passions.

"I'm sorry. I need a moment..."

"Of course."

"You're welcome to look around her...her room. Upstairs, last room on the left."

Mackenzie and Ellington took him up on this offer right away. By the time they were halfway down the hallway toward the stairs, Mackenzie could hear Mike start to sob.

They reached Marie's room and Mackenzie was overcome with the feeling of the place being *lived in.* The fact that the room's occupant would never set foot in it again was haunting.

The room wasn't a mess, not really, but it could have used a good cleaning. There were a few dirty clothes in the floor and clutters of notes and papers on her desk. Mackenzie went to the desk and looked around. She saw lots of notes that were scribbled through, mostly just to-do notes that Marie had made to herself.

She also saw fliers for several different political figures, all the way up to presidential candidates. Some of them were marked up, Marie having made lines and notes as reminders. She had jotted words like *Move to Action* and *Over-sell*, making notes about what made the verbiage on the literature so powerful. It was a perfect little glimpse into what Marie was going to college for—a career in politics.

She saw a small pin—a button people often wore on clothes and hats at rallies—for a local candidate she had never heard of.

"Mr. Totino mentioned that Marie was working with a campaign manager for some politician, right?" Mackenzie asked.

"Yeah. Why?"

She waved her hand at the pile of material. "Marie was very much into this sort of thing. I think we need to talk to the campaign manager she was working with."

Ellington nodded, taking one final look around. As he, too, was about to look through the pile of material on the desk, they heard Mr. Totino call from downstairs.

"Agents? I'm good now…if there are more questions, let's do it now…"

They wasted no time, wanting to get out of the Totinos' hair as soon as possible. They headed back downstairs, where Mike Totino met them in the hallway. "Let's finish up in the kitchen," he said, still wiping tears form his eyes. "Sandra can't do this right now. She's…she's going to be a mess for a while and…shit. Just…let's get through this."

He led them into the kitchen, the house so silent that Mackenzie could hear the hum of the refrigerator.

"Just a few other things," Ellington said, again assuming the lead role. "You mentioned that Marie was working alongside a campaign manager. Do you happen to know who it was?"

"No. Sorry. But it was for a local guy that was running for some position on city council. Neil Rooney."

"So she just assisted? Did she ever head these rallies up?" Ellington asked.

"No. She was too focused on her studies. She usually just assisted. But damn, she was really passionate about this sort of thing."

Mackenzie was interested to see where Ellington would take things next. If she were in charge, she'd wrap it up here. These parents obviously needed some time to properly grieve. Also, it was clear that if there *was* any relevant information to get out of them, it wasn't going to happen right now, so close to having the news delivered. Besides that, they *had* learned a little bit of information—information that was already starting to connect some dots in Mackenzie's head.

She was relieved when Ellington slowly got to his feet. He looked down at Mike Totino with as much empathy as he could muster—a look that broke Mackenzie's heart a bit. "Thank you so much for your time," he said. "We'll leave you alone now. But if you think of anything at all that might aid us in the coming days, please don't hesitate to call the police right away."

"Do you have other family here to come sit with you?" Mackenzie asked as they made their way out, unable to help herself.

"Sandra's sister should be here any minute now," Mike said. "Thank you for checking."

Mike Totino closed the door behind them. When Mackenzie and Ellington were out on the porch, night had fallen. It was bitterly cold, the forecast calling for temperatures to drop below ten degrees that night. It made Mackenzie think of Marie Totino's body in the Patapsco River; it made her hope that the poor woman had been dead before she'd been tossed into those frigid waters.

Neither of them spoke until they were in the car, the heater churning as fast as it could to push out some heat.

"Feel like a dead end to you?" he asked.

"Maybe not. I'd like to see if we can find information on pastimes that Christine and Jo were involved in. We've known since speaking with Charles McMahon that Jo and Christine were both political science majors. And we now know that a third victim also shared that same major."

"So you think our victims are being targeted for their majors?" Ellington asked.

"Maybe not for their majors. But maybe all of these young women had something in common other than their majors. Like advisors in some cases. Or maybe friends. The fact that they were allowing these men to get this close to them…it makes me keep going back to the killer being a friend."

"It almost makes me wish Holland *was* Marie Totino's academic advisor." He thought on this for a moment and then sighed. "Okay, so let's see what other information we can get on clubs or activities that Christine Lynch and Jo Haley were involved in. Man…Deputy Wheeler is really going to start to hate us."

"I doubt it. I think he'd much prefer us throwing more work at him as opposed to having a campus-wide panic over a serial killer."

Ellington nodded as they drove back to the station. She caught him looking in her direction, little side glances to make sure she was feeling okay. Truth be told, she was feeling rather well—much better than she had at this same time yesterday.

To her, that alone was a good sign. Maybe with this one thin thread to potentially link the victims, the end was closer at hand than she could have hoped.

CHAPTER FOURTEEN

When they got back to the station, there seemed to be a very tense mood in the air. Mackenzie noticed that they received a few stares from the officers, some of which seemed to be filled with disappointment. She'd seen similar glares before, usually when local PD started to feel as if a bureau presence was hurting more than it was helping.

"What the hell happened here?" Ellington asked under his breath.

"No clue," Mackenzie answered.

But as she saw Wheeler coming toward them, marching as if he had a trillion things to do, she thought they were about to find out.

"What's going on?" Mackenzie asked.

"The story hit social media about an hour or so ago. And people are already doing their own detective work, making the connections. Three young women—all Queen Nash students—in under two weeks."

"Any idea where the posts originated?"

"It looks like Hazel Isidro posted something on Facebook earlier today and someone made a comment about another body found today, somewhere in a river—but no one had a name. Not yet anyway."

"How bad is it?" Ellington asked.

"Not too bad yet. But we've seen how social media can make things explode out of nowhere. I can pretty much guarantee you that most of the students on campus are going to know about this by morning. Probably even before that."

"What does that entail in terms of police manpower?"

"Extra security, fielding hundreds of calls from anyone that thinks they see someone suspicious. It can get bad. That's why everyone here is on their toes. The chief is on his way to meet with the president of Queen Nash right now to see what can be done to maybe curb the panic."

So much for heading off campus panic, Mackenzie thought.

"Deputy Wheeler, have you been working with anyone specifically at the college to get the information on the victims?" Mackenzie asked.

"A woman at the registrar's office. She's been very helpful."

"I know it's after hours, but we'd like to get as much information as we can on Jo Haley and Christine Lynch. We're particularly looking for any clubs, internships, or assorted groups they might have been involved with."

"It's after hours, so that might take a while."

"That's fine. Oh...and does the name Neil Rooney mean anything to you?"

"Yeah, actually. He was running for city council vice president last November. Why do you ask?"

"Marie Totino was involved in assisting with rallies and fundraisers for him. She was working closely with his campaign manager. I'd like to find out who that is."

"I see. I can get someone to find that information for you. Shouldn't be too hard. There are lots of political science majors that help with things like that come election time. I'm sure it's the same on most campuses that offer the major, but it can get pretty active around here."

"Do any of them ever get out of hand?" Mackenzie asked.

"No. Actually, they tend to be very formal and peaceful. We get a little rumble here and there but nothing like you see on the national news."

"Do you think we—" Ellington started to ask. The ringing of his phone interrupted him. He checked the caller ID, frowned, and then said: "Excuse me a second."

Mackenzie watched as he turned away and spoke quietly under his breath. *That's got to be McGrath,* she thought. And with that thought came another of those odd flutter-like sensations in her stomach.

And this time, she was sure the baby had nothing to do with it.

"Yes sir, hold on," Ellington said. He muted the call and turned back to Mackenzie and Wheeler. "Deputy Wheeler, can you excuse us for a moment? This is our director on the phone."

"Sure. Feel free to use the conference room if you need to."

They walked away from Wheeler and headed to the conference room they had been using as a makeshift office.

"What's he want?" Mackenzie asked.

"I don't know. He said he wants to speak to both of us. I'll just put him on speakerphone."

There were several questions tearing through her head but she knew they were all useless. She'd not have them answered until they spoke with McGrath.

With the conference room door closed behind them, Ellington took the call off of mute and placed it on speakerphone. "Okay, sir," he said as they took seats beside one another. "We're here."

"Thank you," he said. "I'll get right down to it. I sent the two of you there, hoping to get in front of this thing before it became a big campus-wide concern. I'm seeing where word is starting to get out. And with the third victim popping up today, I think I should replace the two of you with someone else."

"With all due respect, why?" Mackenzie asked.

"Because the two of you are too involved. And if it gets out that I had a pair of agents that were recently married and have been romantically involved for months—*and* that they could not close the case—it'll be a circus for the bureau. I made a judgment call in sending you two out together and I'm man enough to admit that it was probably the wrong decision. This has nothing to do with your performance. I asked you to wrap a series of murders in a fairly escalated timeframe.

"But word has barely made it out," Ellington argued. "We were just speaking with Deputy Wheeler. For right now, it's just some commotion on Facebook."

"Which, as you know, means it will be on the eleven o'clock news tonight."

"Director McGrath, we can—" Mackenzie started.

"It's not up for discussion. I want both of you to take a back seat. I want you to remain there, but your role is being demoted. You've worked on it for the last two days so I want you there as resources. I'm sending Yardley and Harrison up there in a few hours, so they'll be active when morning comes and this is a campus-wide thing. And if it gets too out of hand within the first twelve hours or so, I'll send backup."

Mackenzie stood up and started pacing. She was furious, but at the same time, she understood.

"Agents?" he said. "Am I understood?"

"Yes sir," Ellington said, his tone indicating that he really didn't think it was okay at all.

"Before you leave, please make sure the point of contact down there has contact information for Yardley and Harrison."

"Will do," Ellington said, ending the call. He then put his hands on his hips and uttered a curse under his breath.

"He had to," Mackenzie said, though she didn't like the decision any more than Ellington. "He was essentially doing us a favor by allowing us to work this together."

"Still. This thing is about to blow up and *that's* when he takes us off of it?" He fumed a bit before looking straight at Mackenzie and giving her a weak smile. "Then again...if this thing is on campus by morning...if the entire campus knows there's a serial killer out there, that would be stressful as hell for you."

"I'm a big girl. I'd be fine."

Still, the way his anger seemed to flush away when he realized that this might be in her best interest was reassuring to her. Even when it came to his career, he was putting her and their baby over everything else.

"Well, I guess that's that," Ellington said. "I say let's get copies of all of the files and make the best of it."

"The best being what, exactly?" she asked, still a little deflated.

"Being holed up in a room together while two other agents get to face the public outcry in the morning."

"That *is* an interesting way to spin it," she said.

"Come on. Let's go tell Wheeler what's going on."

They left the room together and Mackenzie did her best to hide the fact that she was secretly relieved over the news. Yes, it was terrible to be demoted; it made her feel as if she had done something wrong, that she was somehow inferior.

But the little knot in her stomach that had formed when she knew McGrath was on the phone was growing into something else—something very much like nausea.

Apparently, being pushed to the back seat on the case was making the baby feel a little sick, too.

CHAPTER FIFTEEN

Maybe it was because her hormones were all over the place or maybe it was the knowledge that they were newlyweds…but the first thing Mackenzie and Ellington did when they returned to the hotel was make love. As far as Mackenzie was concerned, it was an amazing way to work out the tension and anger she felt over being given a back seat role in the case. And although she felt a sick stomach a few times, she was able to fully enjoy the moment of it. She also enjoyed the idea that despite being pregnant, their sex life had been nearly unstoppable and unquenchable ever since she'd shared the news with Ellington.

When they were done, they took turns in the shower and by ten o'clock, they had a functional little workspace going within the room. Ellington was set up at the small table by the window while Mackenzie had her laptop and papers spread out on the bed. As she started to look through the case files, she saw via her phone that she had an email from Wheeler. She opened it and saw that he had attached several documents that had come from the university. She opened it and saw that it was the information she had asked for— any clubs or activities Christine or Jo had been involved in.

She read through it and started jotting down notes. "Wheeler got that information for us," she told Ellington as she wrote. "It doesn't look like the girls were part of any of the same clubs, but Jo and Marie did both sign up with an organization that allows students to help with the campaigns of local politicians. They both used it to fulfill some requirement of their majors."

"Nothing on Christine Lynch?"

"Nothing that I can see yet."

"I'm over here looking at the volunteer page on Rooney's site. It's easily accessible and it looks like it's open to just about anyone. The fine print does say that preference will be given to those with political aspirations or an academic background in politics. And it lists the campaign manager as Daniel Humphrey."

"So it's not like these girls had an automatic in," Mackenzie said. "They probably signed up just like anyone else. And at some point, they had to speak with Daniel Humphrey, apparently."

"That might be one of the things we need to find out."

"Is Rooney a Republican or Democrat?"

"An Independent. And from what I can tell, he has quite the following. He lost the election Wheeler was telling us about, but it came much closer than anyone had expected."

"Is there a contact number for Daniel Humphrey?"

"No. Just an email address. I'm going to send one right now."

They fell into silence again as Mackenzie looked over the files Wheeler had sent her. She created a little list of similarities between the girls, finding nothing entirely new. Same major, same interests from what their transcripts and files stated, same year of college. But that's where it stopped. Different academic advisors. Different apartment buildings. From the looks of it, the only strong connection between any of them was the fact that Jo and Marie had both interacted with Humphrey.

Mackenzie then laid out the situations of each girl. It was grisly to think of them in such a way, but when it came to a case with a rushed timeline, it was sometimes the best way.

First victim, Jo Haley. Sex, followed by strangulation. Found in bedroom.

Second victim, Christine Lynch. Sexual activity but no intercourse. Also strangled. Found in kitchen.

Third victim, Marie Totino. Bruise to head and skull fracture. Bound nude, mouth taped. Not clear, though evidence of strangulation.. Discarded in river.

Mackenzie went back and forth over those notes, looking for a story that made sense. She tried to play every scenario out in her head but there was only one that seemed to stick...and even that one felt flimsy.

There's an element of sex to two of them...three if you count the fact that Marie Totino was nude and bound. The one where there is clearly *actual intercourse, the victim was left lying in bed, as if the killer wasn't concerned about leaving any evidence behind. And then the latest was bound and gagged. Those two indicate that the killer might crave power as well as sex—the feeling that he is dominant over his partner.*

Dominance. Power...but a sense of urgency that seems to escalate with each victim.

There was something there...something that Mackenzie couldn't quite grasp. It was like a name on the tip of your tongue, a name her brain could not come up with.

"I'm going to get ready for bed," Ellington said.

Mackenzie nearly said *So soon?* But then she saw the time. Somehow, it had gotten to be 12:10.

"Yeah, good idea," she said. "Even from a backseat view, tomorrow could be hectic."

"I'm surprised Yardley or Harrison haven't called yet."

"I'm not. The one thing Yardley and I have in common is that we hate asking for help. Calling to even check in might seem like weakness to her on the first night. I imagine we'll hear from them early tomorrow."

"More reason to get to bed, then," Ellington said.

They shut down their laptops and got ready for bed. They did even this in a routine-like manner that seemed to foreshadow the years of marriage that waited ahead of them. They climbed into bed and Mackenzie drifted off with Ellington's arm around her, his hand on her stomach. She thought of what was growing beneath that hand and then, inexplicably, she saw Marie Totino in the river, bitterly cold and with her back scraped raw.

And for reasons that were far beyond her, this made Mackenzie cry. She thought of the dead look on Sandra Totino's face as she tried to understand a world where her daughter had been stripped naked, killed, and tossed into a cold river. Mackenzie wept for several minutes, doing her best to keep it in.

She grabbed Ellington's hand, still on her stomach, and he squeezed it sleepily. He pulled her to her and when she realized that he was still awake, turned to him, sank her head into his shoulder, and cried hard. At some point she fell asleep and even though she knew she still had several weeks before the baby started to kick, she could swear she could feel it shifting around in her womb.

**

When she woke up six and a half hours later, the bread crumbs she'd been toying with in her mind the night before were still scattered in her head. Even before she had fully opened her eyes, she started to sort through them again.

Sex. Power. Control.

She then thought of the Totino family and all of the different political campaign literature in Marie's room. At some point, she had likely worked closely with Daniel Humphrey, the campaign manager for an up and coming politician who had nearly pulled off a major upset in a local election for city council.

What must a near-win like that do to the mind of the man who had set it all up? A man who wasn't a politician, but liked to rub shoulders with them?

Power. Control.

68

She got out of bed and walked to the bathroom, where she brushed her teeth and put up her hair. When she walked back out and pulled her laptop out of her laptop bag, Ellington stirred behind her.

"You okay?" he asked.

"Yeah. Just want to check on something."

He sat up in bed and looked over at the clock. Mackenzie knew that he'd feel guilty to see that it was 6:10. He hated to sleep past 5:30 but she also knew that he was also not one to look a gift horse in the mouth. It was extremely rare that they got to sleep in. She was curious to see if he elected to get out of bed or if he'd try to catch a few more hours of sleep.

He decided to roll out of bed. He walked over to her, kissed her cheek as her laptop booted up, and then started his morning routine. Mackenzie smiled, feeling another surge of comfort when she realized just how well they knew one another. On mornings where they weren't rushed, she knew that Ellington spent the first hour or so running through a workout routine and then a shower. The hotel room wasn't very spacious, so when he started his workout—a circuit that included sit-ups, crunches, planks, burpees, and other moves Mackenzie wasn't very familiar with—he did so between his side of the bed and the bathroom door.

As he exercised, Mackenzie started doing some early morning research. She started by looking up Daniel Humphrey's social media accounts. They were all listed as private pages, not granting access to anyone other than those who sent him friend requests. Give that he dabbled in politics, she supposed she understood this. She was about to give up on this route until she discovered that he had two Facebook profiles—one for his professional life and another for his personal life. For the first time, she actually saw the man. He was quite handsome, a thirty-nine-year-old that could easily pass for thirty. While it was indeed his personal profile, it was still quite heavy with political leanings.

She went to his list of friends and quickly scrolled through. The number of females far outweighed the males, and many of them were professional-looking women. A few, though, were cliché selfies, layered with a filter as the women gave sexy little looks and poses to the camera. She went to the search field and typed in the names of the victims.

Jo Haley first. And there she was, listed as a friend of Humphrey.

She tried Marie Totino next and sure enough, she was there, too.

With a small stirring of excitement in her stomach (that was definitely not the baby), she tried Christine Lynch next.

She was listed in his friends, as well.

It was the first solid link between all three victims.

Feeling a lead building around her, Mackenzie then Googled his name but there wasn't much to come up. She then tried typing in Neil Rooney along with his name and got a few more results—namely articles on some of the campaign rallies from last year. Humphrey's name was mentioned in a few articles and he dropped a few lines about how great he thought his candidate was.

From what Mackenzie could tell, the rallies that Humphrey helped to organize tended to draw a much younger audience. Last November, during the campaign in which Rooney had nearly managed to be elected vice president of the Baltimore City Council, he would often play tracks by Rage Against the Machine or Rise Against. Rooney'd quoted a line from *Breaking Bad* during a debate—a moment that had caught national attention for a day or so.

Try as she might, she could not find any stories about violence or altercations at the rallies. It wasn't like he was a presidential candidate or anything; the rallies were usually very small, numbering no more than two hundred or so.

She then quickly Googled Rooney. Right away, she saw that he checked out. He was always on the road, traveling the country. He seemed like a legit guy—like the kind of guy Mackenzie would vote for. He was a professed Christian and he gave money to various charities all around the world. She saw pictures of him visiting Sierra Leone and parts of India, helping the impoverished. She read articles about his perseverance as he stayed by his mother's side as breast cancer slowly killed her.

She was about to give up when one last idea came to her. She typed in the search terms *Daniel Humphrey, Baltimore,* and *crime.*

The first headline that popped up caught her attention. It was such a stand-out that she was sure she would have eventually found it had she continued to dig during her initial search on Daniel Humphrey.

She clicked on the story and read it, still feeling that sense of some sort of foundation being built under her feet—the foundation for a lead. There might be something to it. Maybe…

"What are we looking at?"

She had been so engrossed in her research that she had not heard Ellington get out of the shower and come up behind her. He was dried off and partially dressed—wearing his boxers and buttoning up his shirt.

"Daniel Humphrey," she said. "I was thinking last night...about a killer that goes from strangulation after sex to sloppily disposing a body in a river."

"And what, exactly, were you thinking?"

She took him down the trail, explaining her idea that the killer might be someone who craved not just the sexual aspects of what he was doing, but the control of it all. That's why each murder scene seemed to be less sexually oriented and more about the control of the victim. And when trying to profile a killer based on control, the only people they had really come across that fit that description was William Holland.

"I thought we agreed he was innocent," Ellington said.

"I think he likely is. But then I wondered about this Humphrey guy. I checked his Facebook and found all three of our victims in his friends list. And think about it. Aside from crooked politicians, what other desperate sort of people are going to be power hungry, doing whatever they can do to experience some sort of control—over their lives, over others, and so on?"

"Wannabes," Ellington said. "People, for instance, that might help politicians organize rallies and help with voter sign-up."

"Campaign managers, perhaps," Mackenzie said.

"What about Rooney?" Ellington asked. "Is he clean?"

"He seems like a saint," Mackenzie answered. "Besides, one look at his travel schedule and I'm pretty sure he'd be ruled out anyway. But it doesn't matter...I think Humphrey is where we go next. If he's not our man, he's at least a damn good lead. I found this article," she said, gesturing to her laptop. "It tells the story of a woman that came forward last summer, claiming that three years ago, Humphrey drugged and raped her and one of her friends. She says he threatened to kill them if they told anyone. This woman came forward, claiming that she had been paid off for her silence. She said Humphrey had told her that he could ensure a spot on the team of a politician that is no longer even active so long as she slept with him. They had a relationship for a while but things got toxic. She says the last time they were together, he drugged her and her friend...and then raped them both."

"What about the friend?"

"She never said anything. Nothing from her at all from what I can see."

"Is the woman's story worth believing? Do we know who she is?"

"Her name is Kathy Clements. I haven't had a chance to look her up yet. But this article claims that following the supposed events she claimed to have happened, she quit her job and deleted all of her social media accounts."

"Seems like a bullshit story to me, then." "Same here. But if she was paid off and threatened…maybe these were ways for her to keep quiet."

Ellington shrugged. "Could be. I'll make a call and see what I can find out about her."

He did just that, placing a call to the bureau's resource desk. No sooner had he started speaking to someone on the other end than Mackenzie's phone rang. When she saw the name on the display, she wasn't quite sure how to feel.

It was Yardley. And Mackenzie knew that Yardley was not the type to call for help. So either something had gone very bad or McGrath was throwing another curveball at them. She answered the call, trying to sound as calm as possible.

"Good morning, Agent Yardley."

"Hi, Agent White. Or, well, I guess it's Agent Ellington now, huh?"

Mackenzie cringed a bit. It did sound rather odd. Maybe that was a discussion she and Ellington needed to have in the very near future.

"How is everything going?" Mackenzie asked.

"Decent. I think Deputy Wheeler has us set up about as well as he can. I have all the files and case notes, including all that you left here for us. So thanks for that. Look…with news of the murders circulating around campus, things are a little odd here. Very precarious, you know?"

"I can imagine."

"I was hoping you and Ellington could meet with us sometime today. Maybe around lunch time. We have a few people to interview between now and then."

"Yeah, I think that can be arranged. You need anything else from us?"

"I don't think so. But we can discuss all of that over lunch."

It felt weird to be placed in such a position, knowing there was so much to be done but unable to do the majority of it. As they finished up the conversation, arranging a time and meeting place, Mackenzie felt another of those flutters in her stomach. This time, she knew it was not nerves or any sort of anxiety. Her baby was moving. She'd read about this several times—how even before a bay started to kick, some women might feel what were known as "flutters" as the growing baby grew and shifted.

She smiled, realizing that it was almost like a sign—like her baby telling her that it was okay to take a back seat, given what she was currently going through.

And maybe it was right. Maybe it was time to step aside, to let this new phase of her life properly take over. It was, of course, easier said than done and even as she and Yardley made plans for that afternoon, she couldn't help but feel a little resentful.

When she was off of the phone, Ellington, also freed from his call, looked at her quizzically.

"What's funny?" he asked.

"What? Nothing…"

"You're smiling. Like…almost about to laugh."

"Oh. I…well, I think the baby is moving."

"What? Like kicking? Isn't it too early for that?"

"It is. But this is what's known as *the flutters*. Honestly, it could just be gas."

"Really? You think that's it?"

She smiled again and shook her head. Ellington came to her and wrapped his arms around her. "You think I could feel it?"

"I don't know. It's pretty tiny."

He placed his hand on her stomach anyway, hoping. As he waited, he asked: "Who was on the phone?"

"Yardley. She and Harrison want to meet with us later today."

Ellington made a *hmmm* noise, an indication that for once, Mackenzie was handling an inferior role better than he was. But he said nothing. In fact, neither of them said another word for several minutes as they sat where they were, Ellington waiting to see if he could feel his child move.

In that moment, in Mackenzie's mind, there was no case. It was her and her family. And while the concept of family had always been skewed to her, given how she was raised, it made her heart swell. Her husband, her child…this was going to be her world soon.

It was enough hope and gratitude to make it seem like the world outside had the potential to be perfect, even if just for a single day.

CHAPTER SIXTEEN

They met with Yardley and Harrison at the very same café where they'd spoken with Melissa Evington. It seemed like the most logical spot, as it was in the heart of the student commons. While they all knew that there was concern spreading all around campus, it was not detectable in the commons. Mackenzie wondered if this was namely because in broad daylight, in the center of campus, students felt safe. Even on those manicured lawns and well-maintained sidewalks at night, as they walked to their dorms and apartments, they *should* all feel safe.

It made Mackenzie feel uneasy. She looked around at all of the students within the common area, of all of the females in particular—in the café, in the main walkway, in the lounge, and coming in and out of the resource area—and wondered how many of them did indeed fear the idea of a serial killer but were too proud to show it.

"First of all," Yardley said, "I think it's bullshit that you guys were pushed to the back of this. We've seen the same case files you've seen and have come to the same conclusions as you. We're about to head out to Jo Haley's apartment to have a look around but you know as well as I do, it's not going to lead to much."

"What leads are you currently looking into?" Ellington asked.

"Everything keeps coming back to William Holland," Harrison said. "Something about it doesn't add up. I mean, it doesn't make sense that he'd be the killer, but that's where all the signs are pointing."

"Have to be careful with that," Mackenzie said. "If we arrest anyone on staff at the college now that the story is out, it could be chaotic. And if we arrest him and turn out to be *wrong,* that's going to be bad for the school *and* the bureau."

"Also," Yardley said, "the police have the cell phones belonging to Christine Lynch and Jo Haley. They're both password protected, but they say we should have access to text messages and call histories within several hours."

"Great."

"How about you guys?" Yardley asked. "Anything new?"

"Yes, actually. I found a link this morning, for all three girls. We heard about this local politician, Neil Rooney. A lot of younger voters are getting behind him. But what's more interesting is the story on his campaign manager—a nobody by the name of Daniel Humphrey. Not only does he have Jo, Christine, and Marie all as friends on his Facebook profile, but he's also at the center of a story of an alleged double-rape."

"That *does* add up to a promising lead," Harrison said.

"The downside," Ellington pointed out, "is that all of our key witnesses into the sort of man he is like just happen to be dead."

"Yeah, but we can find more," Yardley said. "What if we can get access to all of the sign-ups on Rooney's website? I assume they'd all have to go through this Humphrey guy, right?"

"I was thinking the same thing," Mackenzie said. "I can do that for you. We can get a list of all of the females that worked for that campaign—particularly female Queen Nash students."

"Wait," Yardley said. "Are you thinking this Humphrey guy might actually be behind the murders?"

"I'm not necessarily saying that. But he's our only link to all three women and his history *with* women isn't the best."

The table fell silent again. It was Yardley, with her abrupt and dry matter-of-fact attitude, that broke it again. "Damn, this is awkward. Just...I don't want the two of you running errands and doing paperwork nonsense for us."

"It's okay," Ellington said, though there was no enthusiasm in his voice.

"Yeah. It's better than being yanked off the case completely and taking requests from you over the phone back in DC."

"So the way I see it," Yardley said, "is that we're sort of in a no-win situation. We go after Holland, and risk making a shitstorm with the college. Go after someone closely linked to the campaign of a local politician and risk pissing off an entire political party."

"Rooney is an Independent," Ellington said with a snicker. "I doubt anyone will mind."

"Jokes aside," Mackenzie said, "we made a formal request. DC is supposed to be sending us some information on the woman that came forward with the Humphrey rape story."

"Honestly," Ellington said, "I don't expect much to come from it. Still, we'll shoot it to you when we get it. The woman seems like the sort that won't mind talking about it *at all*. I'd call her for you myself...but digging into someone's political campaign might be too prominent in McGrath's eyes."

Mackenzie thought Ellington's comment sounded a little barbed. She understood it, though she wasn't quite used to hearing him be so aggressive about being displeased with something.

"No worries," Yardley said. "We can handle it. So it seems to me that you think digging deeper into Humphrey would be a safer bet than going after Holland?"

"I do," Mackenzie said. "While a friends list on Facebook if far from *proof*, it does signify at least some sort of relationship—even if it's a vague or purely digital one."

She felt like she was being far too bossy. She respected Yardley and Harrison as agents, though she didn't know quite enough about them to feel fully comfortable with their approach. She noticed, though, how Yardley seemed to soak up her every word like a sponge and while it was flattering, it also made Mackenzie pick and choose her words very carefully.

"That's where we'll start then," Harrison said. "Right now. And we'll keep you posted every step of the way."

With that, Yardley and Harrison stood up. Harrison, always wearing a satchel-type bag slung over his chest, adjusted it and smiled at them. "Congrats on the wedding, by the way. I hope to God you're not counting this mess as your honeymoon."

"No, we took care of that before this all started," Ellington said, reaching out and taking Mackenzie's hand beneath the table.

Yardley and Harrison smiled a little awkwardly and then headed out on their way.

"You think they're up to the task?" Ellington asked.

"Yeah. Yardley is very determined. And Harrison is extremely task-oriented. It was a smart move to pair them up."

Ellington smiled. "It seems like McGrath has a knack for that, huh?"

"Indeed."

"Anyway, look…I was thinking. I think maybe I'm going to drop you off at the hotel. I'm going to try to swing by and speak to Holland again…see what he knows about Daniel Humphrey."

"I'm fully capable of speaking to Holland, too."

"You are. But of the two of us, who has pissed of McGrath more in the past?"

"Me."

"And who is currently hiding a rather large secret from him?" He asked this question while looking toward her stomach.

"Oh, shut up," she said.

They left moments behind Yardley and Harrison. Mackenzie was surprised just how involved Ellington was trying to be. He was typically the type who obeyed orders, mainly because she knew that he had nothing but respect and admiration for McGrath. She wondered what it was about this case that had him so entranced.

It's because he's about to be a father, she thought. *It's because he has to understand how someone could kill these women without remorse. He has to understand how someone could so easily kill someone's child, no matter how old.*

She wasn't sure if this was correct, but she rather hoped it was. Because one of the things she and Ellington had in common was that when something drove them both professionally and morally, there was no stopping them.

CHAPTER SEVENTEEN

Ellington dropped her off at the hotel, promising to be back within an hour or two. He'd called ahead to Holland, not wanting to seem as if they were trying to surprise him and corner him again. Holland had been reluctant but agreed in the end. Mackenzie figured she could do some more digging into Neil Rooney—maybe even get some names from the higher-ups within his campaign. It might turn out to be a waste of time but with Yardley and Harrison in charge of the case now, there really wasn't much for her to do.

She fired up her laptop again, thinking of a few other avenues she could potentially take. Did Marie Totino have a boyfriend? If so, did *he* perhaps know Christine and Jo? Even that simple sort of link could open up many more possibilities for them.

She had gotten just ten minutes into further digging on Rooney when her phone rang. Not her cell phone, but the ancient-looking hotel phone on the bedside table. The red light lit up, indicating that it was the front desk calling.

She answered it with a sinking feeling in her chest. *Has something happened to Ellington? Has another body been found?*

"Hello?"

"Hi, is this Agent Mackenzie White?"

"It is."

"This is Rebecca from the front desk. You have a visitor down here in the lobby."

"Who is it?"

"They won't tell me. That's why I have not given them your room number. But they are insisting that they speak to you."

She considered her options, trying to figure out who it might be. "Thank you," she finally said. "I'll be down in a few minutes."

She started for the door but then reconsidered. Someone downstairs wanting to talk to her…and they wouldn't give their name…

She grabbed her sidearm and tucked it in the waist of her pants. She covered it up with her jacket and then headed back for the door.

As soon as she opened it, something came speeding directly for her face. By the time she realized it was a gloved fist, she barely had time to duck. Rather than breaking her nose, the punch connected squarely with her brow. She stumbled back, nearly falling before she was able to catch herself on the small sink that sat in the foyer area. Another punch was coming at her and this time she was ready. Still reeling from the first punch, she dropped into a squatting position and kicked her attacker's ankle. As he stumbled forward from the attack, Mackenzie pivoted upward quickly, throwing her elbow out in a greater-than shape. It connected squarely with the attacker's face and she caught a glimpse of his eyes rolling back into his head as he was knocked out.

But another man was already coming in through the door behind him. He was dressed in a white T-shirt and jeans. His face was covered by a simple ski mask. His hands were also gloved. One of his hands held a gun—a basic Glock from the looks of it.

She calculated quickly. Two on one. At least one was armed. No use in engaging in a shootout. One of them was already down. Got to use fists. If you shoot and kill them, you get no information out of them.

Mackenzie seemed to surprise the second man when she charged for him. She cringed, waiting for the shot, but she got there too fast.

That or they didn't intend to kill me…just spook me…

She grabbed the man's arm and swung around hard in an almost comical fashion. His face slammed into the wall. Before he had time to rebound, Mackenzie drew up her knee and crashed it hard into his back. She then used her other arm to reach for her Glock, still waiting at her back.

The man cried out in pain, reaching back for any sort of attack he could muster. His hand found her hair, grabbed a handful of it, and twisted. As he did, he pushed back against her knee. Her scalp seemed to catch fire, taking her just enough off guard that he was able to slip away from between her knee and the wall.

He wheeled around fast and when he collided with her in a hard football tackle, she knew that they had indeed not come here to kill her. The guns were just for show. They had never intended to use them.

As he slammed into her, they both went tumbling backward. Mackenzie struck the side of the bed, managing to finally draw her gun. She bounced off of it and then went falling backward onto the table she had been working at. Her laptop and notes went to the ground as the attacker went for her right wrist, trying to knock her Glock out of her hand. He was brave in his attack, giving up ample opportunity for her to roll away from him while he raised his elbow up and drove it into her wrist.

Mackenzie screamed and was helpless but to let go of the gun. When she did, the attacker perched up to his knees and began to level his gun at Mackenzie's head.

Maybe they weren't expecting this much of a fight, she thought. *Maybe now they'll have no qualms about killing me...*

Before the man could bring his gun all the way up, Mackenzie brought her aching right wrist up and slammed her palm into the side of the man's head. It rocked him but did not get him off of her. Mackenzie bucked and turned to the left, knocking him further off balance. As he flailed for balance, Mackenzie grabbed his right arm and wrenched it down hard. She was trying to snap it but could not get enough leverage to do so. As she scrambled for more of a grip, the man crawled his way backward. He raised his left leg and kicked out. His foot slammed into Mackenzie's shoulder, driving her back. She did not release his arm, though. If she did, he'd have a clear shot at her.

That's when it dawned on her...that she was not the only one in danger here.

My baby...

She wrenched harder, waiting to hear that dry pop of the man's wrist snapping. While that sound did not come, she managed to apply enough pressure to cause him to drop his gun. It clattered on the floor, directly beside her laptop.

Mackenzie lunged for it. Her hand fell on the butt and she drew it close, coming to her knees for the shot.

She was met with another kick.

This one landed squarely along her stomach. The air went rushing out of her and a cry of pain and fear came barreling out of her.

The baby...the baby...

The man came for her again, clearly intending to wrestle her for the gun. With fury boiling inside of her—perhaps feeling a mother's sense of protectiveness for the first time—Mackenzie stopped him with a stiff jab to his chin. She felt two of her knuckles pop, maybe even her pinky breaking, as the man stopped in his tracks, dazed for a moment.

It took everything within Mackenzie not to open fire on the son of a bitch. Instead, she brought a tremendous forearm blow across his neck and fell on top of him as he retched for breath.

"Someone help!" she screamed. "Call—"

She saw the blur of motion too late. The first attacker had gotten up and came rushing at her. He drove a knee into her head. Mackenzie went reeling back, the world going black.

80

Have to hold on…just a bit longer…

The attacker's gun was right beside her. She drew it up just as the first attacker started to raise his.

And then they retreated. The world swayed, went black…

Fuck it, Mackenzie thought.

She fired off a shot. It took every ounce of strength within her to do it.

She was dimly aware that both men were still making a run for it. Her shot had missed. She held the gun up, trying to focus, trying to aim…but everything was swimmy, nothing was stable, and the darkness came rushing on.

When she was confident that the men were gone and not returning, she tried getting to her feet. She then felt her stomach, willing the baby to move, any little flutter to indicate that the kick had not hurt it.

But something in her body—not her stomach but something deep in her heart—told her that she might not want the answer to that right now.

It was this ominous thought that plastered itself to the front of her mind as the darkness finally had its way. She stumbled a moment as she tried to regain her footing and then she fell to the ground, her final thoughts on her baby before the darkness took her down.

CHAPTER EIGHTEEN

She felt movement all around her. She felt someone's hands on her arm, then gently checking her neck. There were voices, but they seemed to be coming from very far away. She heard sirens, piercing wails that seemed to obliterate everything else. She could actually feel them in her bones, in her guts, in her...

"The baby..."

This was her voice, which was good. Hearing her own voice helped to ground her. She opened her eyes and the lights above her made her head feel as if her head was splitting in half.

"You're doing great, Agent White," a man's voice said. This was almost entirely muted by the sirens.

She grinned sleepily and said, "It's Ellington now."

You're in an ambulance, some very rigid part of her mind said. *You just survived an attack against two men and barely escaped. You were kicked hard in the stomach and—*

"The baby," she said again.

"What baby, Agent White?"

The words were on her tongue. As she spoke them, she wondered if it was the best idea. But she had to. Her baby could be in trouble. Her baby could be hurt...or worse.

"Pregnant," she said.

Everything seemed to stop around her: the voices, the movement, even the wailing of the sirens.

"Okay, we'll do what we can," that female voice said again.

"Call Ellington," she said. "The father. He's the—"

But then the darkness came reeling back toward her and she was unable to keep it away.

***

The next time she opened her eyes, the world felt as if someone had placed it on pause. She could tell right away, even before her eyes had fully adjusted to the light, that she was in a hospital room. The smell and the sanitized square shape of everything gave it away. The mattress beneath her bed was somewhere between too firm and just right, and the stillness in the air had that hospital feel to it.

"Mac?"

She craned her head to the right and saw Ellington sitting there. He was out of his seat at once, kneeling by the bed and taking her hand. "How are you feeling?"

It took her a moment to come up with the right words. But even when she had them—*sore* and *scared*—she ignored them. Instead, she asked the only question that she truly cared about.

"How's the baby?"

"We don't know. They're going to do an ultrasound in a few minutes. A doctor did a preliminary check and thinks everything is going to be okay." He paused here and seemed to be keeping his emotions in check. "What happened?"

"Two men with guns. Both wearing ski masks…"

"And you got away? There was a bullet hole in the wall…was that them or you?"

"Me."

"Your left pinky is broken and you have a mild concussion. Do you—"

She shook her head. "Nothing else. Not until I know how the baby is doing."

Ellington quickly glanced to her stomach and then back to her face. "A nurse left here about three minutes ago to roll a machine this way. It should be any minute now."

She nodded and made herself turn away from him. She felt tears coming on—out of fear for her baby, out of her own stubborn nature of not being able to sit on the sidelines when she knew it would be best.

"Mac…can you please tell me exactly what happened? Two men broke into your room and did a number on you. There was a bullet hole in the wall. That's pretty serious stuff."

"Not yet," she said, choking back a sob.

Ellington sighed, resigned.

They remained in silence for another thirty seconds or so when they were interrupted by a nurse wheeling in an ultrasound machine. She glanced quickly at Mackenzie and offered a soft smile. "Hey, you're up! How are you feeling?"

"I need to know about the baby."

"Of course," the nurse said, clearly picking up on Mackenzie's urgency. She kept her head down and worked to get the machine hooked up.

When everything was ready to go, the nurse applied gel to Mackenzie's stomach and started to do a search for the baby. The tension and quiet in the room felt heavy on Mackenzie. She looked to Ellington and noted the stone-like expression on his face. He came to the side of the bed and took her hand. She gave it a squeeze, somehow certain that they were going to receive bad news.

She watched the screen and, after a while, saw the shape of the baby come into view. She'd only had one ultrasound to this point in her pregnancy and despite the fear in her heart in that moment, it still felt quite magical. The moment she saw it, her heart stopped; it was still and unmoving.

And she heard no heartbeat through the machine.

"Hold on," the nurse said, seeing the tension start to sink into Mackenzie. "Your little one is just sort of curled up and hard to get to right now. After all, they had quite a scare. Okay...and here we go..."

The *whoop whoop whoop* of the heartbeat sounded out.

It sounded canned, static-laced, but also beautiful.

"There we go," the nurse said. "Hold on one second and let me check...yes, I don't see any harm done to the baby or to the home you've made for it. Of course, this simple ultrasound can't tell *everything,* though it's a pretty good indicator. We've called the on-call obstetrician. He'll look you over and run a few tests. But based on what I'm seeing, I think you're okay. And extremely lucky."

The nurse cleaned the goo off of Mackenzie's stomach and cleaned the wand. She gave Mackenzie and Ellington a quick nod as she left the room.

When she was gone, Mackenzie could no longer hold in her tears. She let them come freely and when Ellington came to her, sitting on the edge of the bed and taking her in his arms, they came even harder.

But that was fine. She supposed that if a baby could develop to learn its mother's voice from within the womb, it would also learn to understand that every now and then, mommy just needed a good cry.

***

She supposed it could have been worse. She'd come away from the fight with only her left pinky in a very uncomfortable splint and her head was sore from the knee she'd taken and her abs were a little tweaked but other than that, she was fine. The baby, too. Her obstetrician had checked her over and concluded that the baby was fine, though the series of events had likely scared it and caused it to grow tense. It amazed her to think that something that was only fifteen weeks old—*sixteen,* as of today, her doctor had told her—could react to the same sort of environmental factors that she reacted to.

Mackenzie knew without a doubt how lucky she was. She looked over to Ellington, who had stayed in the room with her every moment following the ultrasound. *Yeah,* she thought. *Pretty damned lucky.*

"I think we need to talk about what this could mean," she said.

"You mean why two armed men came in trying to kill you?" Ellington asked.

"Yes. And why it happened once we started looking into Daniel Humphrey."

"I've been speaking with Yardley off and on while the doctors have been seeing you. I spoke with them very briefly when you were first admitted, too. All three of us agreed that it was indeed fishy that you were attacked right after pushing to look into him."

"Are they following up on that?"

"As best they can. And look...you're feeling good now, right?"

"My head is still a little sore. He whacked me pretty good. Why?"

"Well, you might want to know that McGrath is in the waiting room. He's been there for about an hour. I haven't told him anything yet...about the baby. But, Mac....even if we manage to keep it from him while he's here, he'll end up seeing the medical report when it goes across his desk."

"Yeah..."

"Should I send him in?"

She sighed, trying to understand the weight of the situation. She had no idea how he might respond. She was actually quite surprised that he had bothered coming to visit her.

"Yeah, you might as well."

"Want me to be here when you tell him?"

"I appreciate it...but no. Just send him."

Ellington nodded, coming to her bedside to kiss her forehead before heading out to get McGrath.

A feeling of despair went through her. She realized that no matter how McGrath handled the news of the pregnancy—at the fact that she had been hiding it from him—things would be different for her now. For the rest of this case, for the rest of her career, for the rest of her life.

Two minutes passed before McGrath showed up. He knocked politely on the door before walking in. He wore his usual attire of shirt, slacks, and tie but he looked out of place. He looked normal and almost chagrined.

"How are you?" he asked.

"Alive. Lucky." She paused and then added: "If you don't mind my asking…why are you here? It wasn't anything even remotely close to fatal."

"I'm here in the event I needed to run damage control. This attack occurred very close to when you pushed towards looking into Daniel Humphrey. Especially if the two are indeed related…things could get bad. Of course, I also wanted to check in on you."

"You should keep that in mind when I tell you what I'm about to share," she said.

He cocked his head and her heart warmed toward him when she saw genuine concern on his face.

"I'm pregnant. I've known for a few weeks now."

The shock on McGrath's face was only momentary. It was almost instantly replaced with concern.

"Was the baby hurt?" he asked.

"No. I got lucky there, too."

"How far along are you?"

"Sixteen weeks." She looked down at her stomach and shrugged. "It's sort of starting to show."

McGrath approached the bed, his hands on his hips and his head hung low. "Why didn't you tell me?"

"Because I was being stupid and selfish. I figured if I told you, you wouldn't give me any high-profile cases."

"Judging from where you are right now, I'd say that would have been a smart choice."

"I'm sorry," she said. She meant it, too; she meant it so much that she felt tears stinging the corners of her eyes.

"But you're okay?" he asked.

"Yes. Me *and* the baby."

"Good," he said, walking back toward the door. He turned back quickly and added: "And congratulations, by the way."

"Am I in trouble?" she asked, trying to sound funny.

"We'll talk about that later. Get some rest for now."

He left after this, leaving her alone again. Mackenzie wasn't sure how to feel now that McGrath knew. She was relieved and touched because of his reaction. But at the same time, she did not like the lack of control in not knowing her fate.

Several moments later, Ellington reappeared. He came to her bedside and took her hand. "He didn't say much when he came back out," Ellington said. "How did he take it?"

"Much better than I expected. He was genuinely worried about me and the baby. He even congratulated me. But..."

"Yeah, I sensed there was a but."

"I get the feeling I might pay for this. I don't know what he has in mind, but it could be bad."

"You're probably right," Ellington said. "No sense in kidding ourselves about it."

She knew McGrath well enough to know that this was true. The concussion the doctors had diagnosed her with would have been enough for him to seriously push her toward taking a few days off. Add in a pregnancy that had also been in jeopardy, and that's what you call a double-whammy.

"What did he think of the timing of it all?" Ellington asked. "You being attacked when you were, I mean."

"He skirted around that. He did say that was the primary reason he showed up here, though."

"Can I tell you something?" Ellington said.

"What?"

"I'm glad he knows now. At the risk of sounding too cheesy, I'm excited for everyone to know. It makes me happy, and I'm understanding that I'm more excited about it than I realized."

She was happy to hear it, though she had never suspected he'd freak out about it no matter how far along she was. Still, her mind kept going back to the events of the afternoon. The fight itself was nothing more than a blur in her head. But there was one detail that she was still hung up on, something irritating her.

"It all happened because I went to answer the door," she said. She was sure it seemed random to Ellington, but it's where her mind kept tracking back to. "The desk clerk called our room phone and said there was a man downstairs wanting to speak with me. I opened the door to go down there and that's when they jumped me."

"Yardley and Harrison questioned the staff. They got a description of the guy and there's a pretty wide search out for him."

"Good. But there's something else. They had guns. If they wanted me *only* dead, they could have shot me the moment I opened the door. The fact that they just barged in makes me think they wanted me alive. Probably to question me or threaten me."

"And then you kicked their asses and they had to change their plan," Ellington said. He sighed and said, "That's another thing:

McGrath wants your report of how things happened in the next forty-eight hours. He's pressing pretty hard for it. You fired your weapon and there are two men on the loose."

"Maybe when we can get an ID on the guy from the lobby, that'll help."

"Maybe," Ellington agreed. "But that's no longer anything for you to worry about. You're off the case, remember."

She frowned and was about to say something. But then Ellington walked over to her, placed his hand very softly on her stomach, and kissed her on the side of the mouth. "And that's perfectly okay."

She smiled at him but thought: *That's the one thing he doesn't quite know about me yet. Off the case or not, I'll constantly think about it until the damned thing is wrapped.*

And true to form, she was already trying to figure out not only how a supposed nobody like Daniel Humphrey had discovered he was being looked into, but what he truly had to hide.

CHAPTER NINETEEN

Mackenzie drifted off sometime later and woke up to the sound of her phone ringing. It took her a moment to realize that it was not her phone, but Ellington's. When she opened her eyes, he was speaking into it, standing by the door as to not wake her. Something in his voice seemed excited…promising, almost.

She heard him say: "Yeah, I can do that. Soon, yeah." And then he was done.

"Who was that?" Mackenzie asked.

"I was hoping that didn't wake you up," he said.

"Well, it did. Who was it?"

"That was Yardley. They've got tabs on Daniel Humphrey and wanted to know if I wanted to be there. And honestly, I'd like to. I feel like one of us needs to."

"Well, grab my stuff," she said with a lazy grin. "I'll go."

"Ha. Ha. Are you okay if I head out? They've got eyes on him right now, so it shouldn't take long."

In all honesty, she wanted him to stay with her, but that was mainly because the idea of spending another few hours in the hospital alone was depressing. But she nodded, took his hand, and said, "Yeah. Go kick his ass and bring him in. Do it for me and the baby."

Again, she offered a half-hearted smile. But the look in Ellington's eyes was all business. "Oh, I will," he said.

He kissed her softly on the mouth and then walked quickly out of the room Mackenzie watched him go, realizing that she might be getting an early glimpse of what it might be like to have to watch the most exciting part of a case from the sidelines.

***

Ellington sped down the street with about a million thoughts in his head. First, Mackenzie had been hurt and maybe even almost killed. Secondly, their baby had been at risk of also being seriously hurt. And it had all happened on the cusp of looking into this prick Daniel Humphrey. So when Yardley had called and asked if he wanted them to hold off on going in after him, of course he'd said yes.

The drive from the hospital to the area where Yardley and Harrison were staking out the restaurant Humphrey had been seen entering an hour and a half ago took less than twenty minutes. When he spotted their car parked on the side of the street, he parked as close to them as he could. He then took out his phone and called Yardley back.

"I'm three cars behind you," he said. "Is he still in there?"

"Yeah," Yardley said, "nothing new on our end. We've been talking about going in and pretending to be there for dinner. Just to get a better look. What are your thoughts?"

"Give it another half an hour. If he's not out, I'll make up some excuse to go in there and pull him out. Maybe some lie about someone from Rooney's campaign at the bar that wants to meet him."

"Sounds good. How's Mac?"

"She doing great. A concussion and a broken pinky. But it could have been much worse." It took everything within him not to tell her about the baby. Just thinking of revealing the news to Yardley and Harrison made him smile.

"That's great. Let her know we would have loved to have been there but we were hunting down this creep."

They ended the call, leaving Ellington to stare out the window at the high-end restaurant Yardley and Harrison had been parked in front of for over an hour already. He wondered just how closely tied to Mackenzie's attack this Humphrey jerk was. He wondered how much the attackers had been paid and what sort of campaign fund Humphrey had swiped the money from.

He suddenly wondered if it had been a mistake to come out and take part in his arrest. If he didn't calm down a bit, he was afraid his temper—which he usually did a reasonable job of keeping in check—might get the better of him.

Exactly eleven minutes after he arrived, he saw that he was going to get the chance to test out the rein on his temper. He watched as three men and a woman came out of the restaurant, one of whom was clearly Humphrey. The canopy lights of the restaurant's little canvassed walkway shone down directly on them so there was no mistaking the man he had seen in serval pictures since they'd started looking into him.

His phone dinged as he received a text from Yardley. **That's him. We'll move with you the moment you open your car door.**

To Ellington, it looked like Humphrey was waiting on the valet to bring his car around. Not seeing the point in waiting for the car to arrive, Ellington got out of the car. He walked quickly toward the restaurant, taking note of Yardley and Harrison joining him, falling in behind.

They crossed the street and approached the group of four people. Only one of them seemed aware that they were being approached. It was the woman, dressed in an elegant and slightly slutty black dress. She nonchalantly grabbed Humphrey's shoulder and said something to him. He turned, saw the agents walking toward them, and his eyes got rather wide.

"Mr. Daniel Humphrey?" Ellington asked.

"Who's asking?" Humphrey said. He was tall and a little overweight but still had something of an intimidating figure. It helped that he carried himself like he thought he was royalty.

"Agent Ellington, with the FBI. I'd like to have a moment of your time, please."

"About what, exactly?"

"Things I don't think you'd want discussed in front of your companions. Just five or ten minutes, that's all I ask."

"I really don't have time."

Ellington stepped forward. Harrison followed, keeping his distance, but flanking to his right. Yardley stayed where she was, watching it unfold and ready to act if needed.

Standing within three feet of Humphrey, Ellington dropped his tone to just above a whisper. He leaned in close and said: "Given that your name has come up in a recent string of murders *and* that I highly suspect you sent people to bully my wife today, I suggest you make the fucking time."

"Or what?" Humphrey said. It was clear that he had long grown accustomed to thinking he was as powerful and influential as the people he rubbed shoulders with. Ellington wondered just how many favors had been granted to this twerp because of the people he knew.

"Or I'll arrest you right here in front of this pretentious restaurant." He leaned in closer, his mouth nearly to Humphrey's ear now, and added: "And I'll make sure to bend your arm back just enough to make you squirm in front of your woman right here. Take your pick. And choose wisely, please. If I'm being honest, I'm looking for a reason to drop your ass to the ground."

Humphrey looked back to his three friends, giving them a *what are you gonna do* look. "Could you guys grab the car for me and just meet me down the street?"

The woman nodded as Humphrey turned away and looked to Ellington. "Fine," he said. "Lead the way."

Ellington did, leading him back to the car that Harrison and Yardley had been sitting in. Without being asked to do so, Harrison and Yardley took the back seat, allowing Ellington and Humphrey to sit in the front. When all four of the doors were closed, Humphrey instantly went rigid. Ellington could see the man's nerves in his eyes—not necessarily an indication of guilt, but that he had never quite been treated in such a way.

"So what murders are you even talking about?" Humphrey demanded.

"Three murders, all young women that we believe are in some way related to the Rooney campaign you helped to run last fall. You are the only link between the three of them, and you're friends with all of them on Facebook."

"That's your link?"

"Well, that and your questionable history with women."

Humphrey looked as if someone had reached out and slapped him in the face.

"Mr. Humphrey, do you recall ever meeting women by the name of Jo Haley, Christine Lynch, or Marie Totino?"

The look spread across Humphrey's face again. This time, it was even stronger. It was like watching someone trying to take in far too much information at once. It made Ellington very uneasy because no matter how good of an actor this man might be, Ellington was pretty sure his shock was genuine.

"Marie Totino?" he asked, the name seeming to fall out of his mouth.

"Yes."

"You're sure?"

"Positive. Her body was discovered in the river yesterday. The third woman in the area in less than ten days. I take it you knew her?"

Humphrey nodded, the look of shock now morphing into confusion. "We…we sort of went on a date. Two dates, actually. That was sometime back in…I guess it was October."

"A date? What was the age difference?"

"I don't know. Eighteen or nineteen years, maybe."

"How did the date go?" Yardley asked from the back.

"Well enough. It was dinner. Two dinners. I tried to kiss her on the second date, but she wasn't interested."

"Did you speak to her again after that?" Ellington asked.

"I tried texting her a few times, but she never responded."

"How did you meet?"

"It was at one of Neil Rooney's fundraisers. It was like a dinner event. We talked for a very long time about minority votes. I remember because she was so passionate about it."

"What about the other women? Lynch and Haley?"

"I don't remember them. I assume they are my Facebook friends because I may have met them at some event or another."

"Do you make a habit of picking up women at campaigns?" Ellington asked. "It's not the noblest thing, but if we knew that for sure, it would answer some questions."

Humphrey was clearly embarrassed when he nodded his head. "Yes. That's how I got Marie's number."

"Off of some sort of registration list?" Harrison asked.

"Off of the sign-ups to help with the campaigns. Me and another guy would put a little mark by women we found attractive. We'd make a point to hit them up after an event…make promises about letting them meet higher-ups…politicians, people in power."

"Classy," Ellington said. "Did it work?"

"Yes, a lot of the time. But…I don't know. I sort of grew out of that. When Marie made me feel a little pathetic and unwanted…I started to realize how sad it was."

"Based on what you're telling me, I'm going to ask you for alibis on the nights these three women were believed to have been killed."

"You said it was over the course of the last ten days or so?" Humphrey asked. There was a flicker of hope in his voice.

"Yes. Ten or eleven days."

"Let me know the dates and I can give you my schedule. I've been all over the place recently. I just got back from DC three days ago. I was there for two days. Before that, I was in Raleigh, North Carolina, for a few days."

"Can you provide proof of that?" Ellington asked.

"Not this very second. But I can get you enough to ease any suspicion within an hour or so."

"So I'm just supposed to let you go?"

"No way," Yardley said from the back. "Mr. Humphrey, my partner and I are going to follow you. Any proof you have, you can hand over to us. Agent Ellington, I believe you have other, more important places to be."

Ellington gave Humphrey a long stare before opening his door to head back to his own car.

"Agent…?" Humphrey said.

"What?" Ellington snapped.

"If I provide a tip…it's supposed to be anonymous, right? Like you can't tell a suspect who it was exactly that called them out, right?"

"Unless it is absolutely necessary to break that confidence. Why?"

"Well…the other man that marked the names on the sign-up lists isn't exactly the definition of integrity, either. I wouldn't say he's capable of murder but then again, I don't know him all that well."

"Give me a name."

"Bruce Dumfries. He's a lobbyist that tends to step on toes. Stays quiet, though. But he was always at those events. We…well, we sort of worked together when it came to trying to pick out women. He's sort of a creep, you know?"

"I'll look into it," Ellington said, restraining himself to not call Humphrey a name in return. "As for now, please be cooperative with these two agents. You make one sign of trouble for them and you *will* be arrested."

He didn't even wait for a response or to watch Humphrey get out of the car and head back over to his friends who, even then, were just now getting into Humphrey's car. A large part of Ellington wanted the so-called alibis to fall through. He wanted the case to be over so he could get Mackenzie back home safely. Because if he knew anything about his wife, it was that she would not stop until the case was closed—no matter the cost.

The hell of it was that his gut told him that Humphrey was not their man. Otherwise, he would not have come to the car so easily and he certainly would not have offered up alibis so quickly.

He quickly typed the name Bruce Dumfries into his Notepad app and then started his car. He turned it back to the hospital, his thoughts once again going back to solely his wife and his unborn child.

A wife and child who were, in his eyes, at risk of danger until they returned back home.

CHAPTER TWENTY

Mackenzie was staring at an old action flick on TV when Ellington came back into the hospital room just before ten o'clock. She was not really watching the movie, though; she was far more distracted by details of the case, wondering how every possible scenario might play out in her head. It was all she could think to do now that she was not actively involved with the case.

When he came to the side of the bed, he took her hand right away and sank into the visitor's chair. "How are you?"

"Good. I signed the last of the discharge papers about half an hour ago. We're good to get out of here. I got pain meds for my head and finger. And I've been advised to travel as little as possible for the next day or so on account of the concussion. So it looks like I'm not only going to be useless from here on out, but I'll be stuck in a hotel room."

What she didn't dare tell him was that she was relieved at this last wish. It meant she would be in the area for at least another ten to twelve hours, able to keep tabs on the progress of the case.

As she got out of bed and started sorting through her personal items, she tried to seem as disinterested as she could. "Did you get to Humphrey?"

"I did. Got to talk to him up close and personal. But no arrest. He didn't put up too much of a fight and he says he has alibis for the last few days. Yardley and Harrison are tailing him until he can provide solid evidence of those alibis." He then went on to tell her about the admitted history between Humphrey and Marie Totino.

"Seems suspicious," Mackenzie said.

"I thought so, too. But he admitted to using campaign assistant sign-ups to target women he thought were hot. He said there was another man that helped him do it, some lobbyist named Dumfries."

"Anyone looking into him?"

"I spoke with McGrath on the way here. He said he'd start looking into it for now and wants me to run with it as soon as we get you back to the hotel."

Mackenzie didn't say anything else as they underwent the process of checking out of the hospital. She didn't want to seem like a spoiled brat who wasn't getting her way by not taking an active part in the case. But she also didn't want to ask a trillion questions and come off as being needy. The way she figured it, Ellington would fill her in when it was appropriate.

Still, she found herself lost in thought as Ellington completed the drive back to the hotel. She thought of the organizational structure of a political campaign in particular. She wondered why someone like Daniel Humphrey decided to help organize campaigns and rallies for politicians rather than *being* a politician himself. Sure, there had to be a desire for power there, but it was almost like a passive sort of power...like watching someone powerful from afar.

Maybe even someone that takes pleasure in doing favors for people in power, Mackenzie thought. Someone just like a lobbyist, the very sort of man Humphrey claimed had helped him cull the sign-up lists for young women.

As they pulled into the hotel parking lot, Ellington received another call. Mackenzie frowned at this, knowing full well that at McGrath's instruction, Yardley and Harrison would not be calling her for assistance. And because Yardley and Harrison were now on the case, Deputy Wheeler would not be reaching out to them, either.

She listened to Ellington's side of the conversation as he parked the car. He stayed in the car as he finished up, Mackenzie listening in and trying to figure out the context of the conversation. She felt tired and it was rather hard to concentrate. She figured it was another result of the concussion—a concussion the doctor had said was not too severe but nothing to be taken lightly, either.

He was off of the phone three minutes later. He didn't even both reaching for the door handle, knowing that Mackenzie was going to want to be filled in.

"A couple of things," he said. "That was Harrison. They've got a pretty perfect still frame of the guy that came into the hotel asking for you. No ID match yet, but they expect one within a few hours. Second thing...Humphrey has more than enough to back up the fact he wasn't in Baltimore when these women were killed. Plane tickets, receipts from restaurants and bars in DC. He says there's also several people we could call that can confirm he was there as well."

"So now we start going after this Dumfries character?"

"Bruce Dumfries...yeah. But...you said *we*. I'm pretty sure McGrath would have me hanged if I let you help me on it."

"Probably." She wasn't necessarily upset with him over McGrath's decisions, but she *did* feel a bit like a child because of the intense jealousy that went spiraling through her. "It just sucks. I

96

know it sounds immature, but that's the best way to put it. I was attacked. The fact that I won't be present to nail whoever was behind it stings a bit."

They walked to the hotel room hand in hand. When they got inside, Mackenzie felt the need for a shower—to get the fight off of her, to get the hospital stay off of her. And then she was going so rest. She figured that because she was now off of the case and injured (*and*, she thought, *let's not forget pregnant*), she might as well just sleep until Ellington woke her up and told her it was time to go back to DC. What better way to keep a case from itching at her than to sleep through its inevitable conclusion?

You're depressed, she told herself as she started to undress. *The pregnancy is making you overreactive...the emotions, the hormones, the fact that you fought off two armed men...it's a lot.*

She figured she *was* depressed. The only light at the end of the tunnel was that it sounded as if the case was moving in the right way. With a lead like Daniel Humphrey falling through the cracks, it was hard not to feel a little hopeless.

"I'm getting in the shower," she said. "Will you still be here when I get out or are you rushing over to the precinct?"

"I should still be here." He gave her a once-over as she walked into the bathroom in noting more than her underwear. "I mean this in a strictly helpful sense, you having a concussion and all. But do you need help?"

She smirked at him. "No, I think I'll be fine."

He watched her until she turned the water on and stepped into the shower. The feel of his eyes on her always made her feel a little invigorated but even that did very little to lift her spirits. She stood under the water for a while, letting the steam soak into her, before she slowly washed off. As her hands passed over her stomach, she looked down to it with a frown.

Sorry, she thought. *We had a close call today. And that's on me. Mommy promises to be smarter from here on out. But hey...you already survived your first shootout...so that's exciting.*

For reasons she could not quite understand, this little semi-telepathic conversation with her baby put a smile on her face. She could totally understand how some women claimed to have felt a link to their babies from just a few weeks into the pregnancy. And for now, if she needed to, she knew she could rely on her new duty of being a protective mother to help get her through her lack of action at the end of this case.

***

Ellington headed out shortly after midnight. Mackenzie could tell that he was feeling guilty about having to leave her behind so she hid her own feelings of feeling left out as best as she could. She lay in bed, staring into the dark and trying to sort out her place in it all. They had been checked into a new room and profusely apologized to for what had happened earlier in the day. It had added just one more surreal exclamation point to the day.

That's just it, she told herself. *You have no place in this. This is not your case any longer. Sit back and watch everyone else wrap it up.*

It was sound advice, but everyone else had not endured an ass-kicking and managed to fend off two armed men. As immature as it might seem, Mackenzie could not let that go. She was taking it personally now and felt that she had the right to come face-to-face with not only those two men again, but with whoever had sent them after her.

It was next to impossible for her to go to sleep, knowing that while she was lying here, feeling useless, three agents she worked with (and one she was particularly intimate with) were in the process of trying to wrap a case that now seemed as slippery as ever. She would have given anything to have access to a live feed of the precinct, just to stay abreast of everything.

Her laptop had been cracked during the fight earlier in the day, so even if she wanted to pull up the case files, she wouldn't be able to. She was literally stranded in this motel room with only the television to keep her company.

She went to her suitcase and dug out the bottle of melatonin she sometimes packed on trips. It had been especially helpful back when nightmares of Nebraska had haunted her and ever since then, she had not had to rely on it much. But she took it now, desperately wanting sleep to take her away from several hours.

But even then, half an hour later when she felt the drug starting to take effect, the case was still on her mind. Something about the profile of the killer continued to throw her off. The mix of power and caution, of dominance and inexperience. It made for an interesting mix and the more she thought about it, the harder it was to come up with a fitting profile. Daniel Humphrey did indeed seem to fit her profile but now that he was out of the picture where did they go from here? Looking for a man who craved power and got it by rubbing shoulders with those who wielded it rather than seeking it out for himself?

There's something there, she thought. *Something about power and his inability to grasp it. But what?...*

It was a question that rang out just soon enough for her to regret taking the melatonin. As it was, she could only grasp for the thought like a drowning woman at sea just before the crashing waves of sleep swept her away.

CHAPTER TWENTY ONE

When she woke up the following morning, she didn't even waste time getting out of bed or brushing her teeth. She sat up in bed, picked up her phone, and called Ellington. She figured there must at least be some form of lucrative line on Bruce Dumfries or else he would have returned to catch some sleep. That, or he had been unfortunate enough to get caught up in the monotonous task of verifying all of Humphrey's alibis.

After the fourth ring, she expected the call to go to voicemail, so she was quite happy to hear his voice when he finally answered.

"Good morning, beautiful," he answered.

"Same to you. Late night?"

"Yeah. In looking into Bruce Dumfries, we found out that he and Holland seemed to have once been friends So we did some digging there as well. I'm headed back out to talk to him later this morning. That man is going to be tired of seeing me."

"What do we know about Dumfries?"

"There's not much on him. He donates money to causes that are mostly left leaning, though he has some support on the right side of the aisle. He seems like the kind of man that keeps quiet. Does all of his work in the shadows, not wanting attention."

"So what happens now?" Mackenzie asked.

"I suppose I'll end up paying a visit to Bruce Dumfries. I'm hoping my visit to Holland will at least give me some direction, though; for right now, the only link between Dumfries and the victims is the fact that Humphrey called him out."

"Sounds like a wild goose chase," she commented.

"Feels like one, too. So...yeah. I'm going to finish up here. Some paperwork, last-minute stuff with Wheeler, and then pay Holland a visit. If I have time, I'll go chat with Dumfries. I think McGrath might be okay if I had to stay all day on that. But after that..."

"Then back home?"

"Yeah. And if your noggin is feeling better, maybe I can finally carry you across the threshold."

"Sounds like a plan," she said. But she knew he was likely detecting the disappointment in her voice. If he did, he said nothing about it.

"See you in a bit," was all he said. "Love you."

"Love you, too."

She sat on the edge of the bed for a moment, considering her options. She could remain where she was like a good little girl and just wait for everyone else to do the work. She knew that's what she *should* do.

But something felt wrong...something felt *off*.

She thought of a man like Humphrey, craving power so badly that he would essentially become a lapdog for someone who hadn't yet even become powerful—someone like Neil Rooney who just had a following. Maybe she had been wrong in coming up with a profile. Maybe someone like Humphrey, craving power from a secondary standpoint, wouldn't be capable of murder. To kill someone, you had to *take* control. You had to be confident enough to make that decision and wield that dark power.

It didn't fit with a man who made his living as a lobbyist like Dumfries, either, though. Lobbyists tended to support others, to often throw money at causes to help those causes gain control. Unless the control came from actually *giving* the money and feeling the cause owed you. It was an interesting line of thought for sure.

She stopped thinking of potential suspects for a moment. Instead, she revisited Christine Lynch's apartment in her head. She saw the political science textbooks and biographies on the shelves. She then thought of her time spent in Marie Totino's bedroom—the fliers, brochures, even the little campaign button.

What am I missing? What did we not see?

She then tried to apply all of that scattered evidence to what they knew of the case so far: the similarities, the links, the leads that had come to nothing.

Slowly, she got up. She had a plan—a plan that Ellington was not going to like. A plan that McGrath would *certainly* disapprove of.

She looked down to her belly and rubbed it. "It's okay, baby. There's no harm in this. This is safe."

She went to Ellington's suitcase, hopeful that she'd find what she was looking for. While he wasn't very organized at heart, he was a creature of routine. She knew that he liked to pack extras of certain equipment—an extra clip for his gun, a backup badge, two flashlights, an extra lock-pick set.

She found the lock-pick set stuffed in beside the extra flashlight. She imagined these items remained in his suitcase at all times, never even getting unpacked. She wondered how long it had been since this kit had even been touched. She checked it over, made sure that everything was present and accounted for. She tossed the kit on the bed and then called a cab company; she was told her ride would be there in about fifteen minutes.

She then dressed quickly, brushed her teeth, and readied herself for the day. *Three hours,* she thought. *That should be plenty of time. Very doubtful Ellington will be back before then.*

She tried to talk herself out of it, tried to tell herself that she needed to think of the best interests of her career…of the best interests of her baby.

But it did no good. After all, what would she tell her baby if she let this notion go and a killer remained at large?

You should call Ellington, she thought. *Tell him what you're thinking.*

But she knew that would cause tension and, ultimately, have him deny her. He was thinking like a husband and a father right now. He'd shoot it down and while he might pass it along to Yardley and Harrison, she'd feel better handling it herself. Besides…it was like she had told her baby moments ago. There was no danger where she was headed. She'd likely be back in this hotel room within an hour and a half.

Before she could change her mind, Mackenzie left the room and headed down to the lobby. She did so on high alert, not quite convinced that there wouldn't be someone else lurking around a corner to get another jump on her.

When she got outside, her cab had just pulled up. She got into the back, gave the cab driver the address, and tried to stamp down the guilt that wrapped around her heart.

***

Mackenzie wasn't sure if she needed to check her conscience or if she was beginning to develop looser morals than she had when she'd joined the FBI. The sensation of guilt had faded during the cab ride and by the time she was picking the lock to Christine Lynch's apartment, it was gone completely. In fact, as the tumbler turned and the lock clicked, she felt a rush of excitement.

She stepped into the apartment and had a look around. She skipped the kitchen, heading directly for the book case in the living room. She scanned the titles but found nothing of interest. But she then looked back toward the kitchen, feeling that maybe she *had* seen something but had overlooked it.

She went back into the kitchen, stood against the counter, and had a look around. She scanned the small area slowly, taking it all in. It took about fifteen seconds before she recognized the significance of something that had been placed on the refrigerator with a magnet. She stepped to the fridge and saw a flier that was very similar to some of the ones she had seen in Marie Totino's bedroom. She took it down and looked it over. She was not too surprised to see that it was a flier from the last election cycle—a flier promoting Neil Rooney. She opened it up, read through it, and sure enough, there was Daniel Humphrey's name at the bottom, listed as campaign manager.

There were a few quotes in the flier, some from politicians that Mackenzie had actually heard of, all praising Rooney. Mackenzie read the entire thing from cover to cover and then made her way into Christine's bedroom. She stood at the doorway, taking in the scene in the same way she'd done at the kitchen. A bed to the left, a closet to the right. A dresser straight ahead, a desk tucked into the left corner of the room by the window.

She took her time, checking around the place. She looked in the single drawer within the bedside table and found nothing of interest. She then looked over the desk. Everything was sorted and neat, the mail tucked away in a small basket, her entire laptop set-up wireless and uncluttered. The drawer beneath the desk contained only notebooks and old papers she had written for school.

She then looked to the top of the dresser. There was a lamp, a jewelry box, and a single book sitting on top of it. The book was fiction, the latest Nicholas Sparks title. The jewelry box was opened, everything given its proper place inside. The only exception was a single item that had been set out, as if set aside on purpose. Not being in the box and given its own little place, it looked very much out of the ordinary within Christine's extremely tidy room.

Mackenzie picked the trinket up and looked at it. It took her a while to understand what it was. It looked like the sort of gold lapel pins that pilots sometimes wore, only bigger. It was in the shape of a scroll-style ribbon, about three inches across and two inches tall. In the center, a simple message had been engraved:

ERIC CONNOR
Support VIP

Eric Connor was a name that Mackenzie recognized. She wasn't exactly well-versed in the field of politics, but she'd heard the name enough around DC. She was pretty sure he was a fairly well-loved senator. And apparently, Christine had been given this special little token for supporting him.

Something else occurred to Mackenzie as she held the pin. She made her way back through the apartment, to the kitchen. She looked at the Neil Rooney flier one more time, opening it up to where people were quoted speaking about Rooney. The very first quote came from none other than Eric Connor.

"Neil is not only a friend of mine, but someone I respect and admire greatly. I've gotten to watch him grow, right along with his tremendous ideas and his great love for this country. Keep your eyes open, America! Neil Rooney is going to be doing some very great things."

She thought for a moment, traveling back in her mind to when she had gone looking through Marie Totino's room. She'd had some literature on Rooney as well. And apparently, Rooney and Connor were friends. And that meant, by way of association, Daniel Humphrey was also more or less connected to Eric Connor.

She checked her watch. She'd already been away from the motel for nearly forty-five minutes. To call a cab and ride all the way to the Totino residence would be pushing it. She took a while to properly think out the idea that was slowly dawning on her and realized that if she had already come this far, there was no sense in stopping now.

The guilt started to creep back in once again as she pulled up the number she had been given for Mike and Sandra Totino. As the phone rang, she went over some of the victims' similarities again, for what seemed like the millionth time. But now, after seeing the pin and the flier in Christine's room, things started to feel a little more solid—a little more like a path that might lead somewhere worthwhile.

They're all connected to a campaign for Neil Rooney, which was organized and set up by Daniel Humphrey. They are all ardent political fans; they all attend rallies and are political science majors. They were all very much get-out-and-vote women. Even if Daniel Humphrey is innocent, maybe there was someone else. Someone like Bruce Dumfries.

Mike Totino answered the phone, breaking her train of thought.

"Hello?" He sounded worn out…tired.

"Mr. Totino, I am so sorry to bother you again. This is Agent White. I have a very quick question I was hoping you could answer for me."

"I can try," he said. She also realized that his voice sounded raspy. He'd been crying recently and likely not getting enough sleep.

"I'm wondering if there has been any time in the last year or so where Marie was involved in something with a senator named Eric Connor."

"I'm not sure…I think…I think maybe she was. I seem to remember that name. It might have been that event or gala or whatever that she went to sometime last summer. It was for someone really big in DC. Pretty sure it was a senator, but I'm not positive."

"Do you remember her maybe going to this event with someone else?"

"Oh, no. She was a loner for that sort of thing. She always said anyone going to a rally or event like that in a group was not going for the right reasons. You know…now that I think of it, this event she went to…the one she was so excited about…she brought something back with her. Some little thing she was showing off to us and some of her friends."

"Like a gift?" Mackenzie asked.

"No, nothing like that. Just a little gold button."

"You mean like a pin?"

"Yeah, like a pin you wear on your shirt or jacket. I remember her saying only people they allowed backstage got one."

"Backstage?"

"Yeah, I'm pretty sure that's what she said. It all…well, it's all sort of muddied. And it makes me realize now, after she's gone, that I never really paid much attention to what she wanted to do with her life."

Mackenzie had no idea what to say to that. She had never been great at consoling people and here, on the phone in a dead woman's apartment, surely wasn't going to be the moment she started.

"Does that help?" Mike asked.

"Mr. Totino, I think it just might."

"Good," he said. He hung up then and the clicking noise in Mackenzie's ear seemed far too loud.

She looked at the pin in her hand. One that Christine Lynch must have also gotten backstage at some event for Eric Connor. She wondered if Jo Haley had a similar pin and if so, where it might be.

I don't have time to go rummaging through Jo Haley's apartment, too, she thought. *This is one of those cases where I might just have to make an assumption.*

And it would be a good one, she thought. All three women had ties to Daniel Humphrey, and Humphrey worked closely with Neil Rooney, who was also friends and perhaps a student of sorts to Eric Connor. It felt very much like some deranged version of Six Degrees of Kevin Bacon. And somewhere in there was Dumfries...a man who seemed to remain private and in the shadows.

What might he be hiding in those shadows? she wondered.

Fully aware that she was breaking a rule, she pocketed the pin and called the same cab company she had used before. As she waited, she went back into the bedroom and had another look around. She went through the jewelry box, just in case, wondering if there was some other trinket in there. She looked under the bed for any books or loose documents. She thumbed through the papers and notebooks in the desk...and found a loose scattering of what looked to be discarded papers—the same sort that seem to collect in forgotten drawers and closets in every home.

She took them out from between the college papers and notebooks. There was a stack of such papers about one inch thick. Even Christine's clutter looked organized, the papers folded nearly in half and tucked into one another. As she unfolded the papers, she saw old notes for her college papers, an invitation to a wedding from a year ago, and a birthday card from her sister.

She then came to a sheet of paper that had very clearly gotten wet at some point and then dried out. The majority of the paper could not be read, having been soaked and nearly crumbled apart.

It was an invitation to a fundraiser and gala event for Eric Connor. The event was held last September and referred to the invited, Christine Lynch in this case, as a *VIP supporter.*

Christine was at this event. Marie was there, too. One hundred bucks says Jo Haley was also in attendance.

She further scanned the document and at the very bottom, in fine print along the bottom of the footer, was a *Special Thank You* section. There were several names there, some the names of companies, but mostly the names of individuals. And it was there, mixed in with all of the other names, that she spotted Bruce Dumfries.

She was now quite comfortable in adding him to the chain of potential suspects, shoving him in right behind Humphrey. Sure, his alibis might have checked out, but he fit her profile so perfectly, it was hard to ignore him completely.

How would Dumfries be involved with this campaign, other than offering up money to some cause that Senator Connor was behind?

She had no time to find out.

Her brain kicked into overdrive as she thought through it all. But before she could get anywhere, her phone rang, startling her. She saw that it was the cab company; it was time to go back to the hotel.

She went downstairs and climbed into the back of the cab. When the driver asked for a destination, it took every bit of restraint within her not to give him the address she had on file in her emails for Jo Haley. Instead, she reined it in and asked to be taken back to the hotel. As she did, she touched the golden pin in her pocket, realizing that she was going to have confess her little journey to Ellington.

She supposed it would be just as good of a reason as any to have their first marital spat.

CHAPTER TWENTY TWO

If he was going to keep doing this, he knew he had to be more careful. There were three so far. *Three.* He'd thought that disposing of Marie in the river would relieve him, would help him to feel less stress. And while the authorities were nowhere near catching on to him, he knew he could not get cocky.

After all, the story was in the news now. It was circulating around campus. And as he watched the late-night news programs from his warm living room, he saw that the authorities *had* managed to come up with a few leads. They were all dead ends, especially the misguided investigation into Neil Rooney's campaign manager, a poor sap by the name of Daniel Humphrey.

And while the authorities were way off base, it did show that they were very much dedicated to solving his crimes.

Ah, not that it mattered. There was only one other woman out there, one woman who knew too much. Once he disposed of her, his task would be over and he could resume his normal life.

When he picked up his phone and started to send a text to her, he realized that he was excited. He had grown to like the act of murder. Well, maybe not *like*...it more like a stark appreciation. And he was apparently quite good at it. It nearly made him sad that this would be the last. Of course, he supposed if he really wanted to do it again in the future, there would be nothing to stop him.

Stop worrying about the future, you fool, he told himself. *You still have one more right now. Why don't you go ahead and take care of that one first?*

He did just that, composing the text and then sending it. He was getting excited, growing aroused as he pressed send. And not because of the implications of what was in the text, but because he knew the real reason behind it. That she, too, would die at his hands.

It's been far too long, he typed. **I think I could do for some breakfast.**

He set the phone down and waited. These women...these younger women who had barely even broken into their twenties— were always quick to respond. He knew it wasn't only because they were so eager to please him. No, it was something about this poor generation…always needing to be up to date and in the know.

Sure enough, his phone buzzed at him. It was not his standard phone but one of those cheap drug store deals. He went through them regularly in the event of someone's carelessness. Perhaps his own. Perhaps one of his girls'.

Early class in the morning, silly. Dinner?

No, he responded. **I'm busy all day after lunch.**

Shame. I'm HUNGRY too.

He smiled. It was almost too easy. He was beyond excited now, sensing the finality of it. The woman typing this…she had very little time to live. And he was the only one that knew it.

After your class? he suggested. **At the old spot?**

I can do that. 10:00?

Can't wait, he sent.

And he meant it.

With Jo, he'd given in to his most base desires. They had slept together and in the middle of it, knowing what he had to do before the night ended, he went ahead and killed her. Strangling her had been harder than he had anticipated; he blamed the fact that he had been more interested in the sex for far too much of the night.

That was why he had opted to forgo sex with Christine and Marie. He could not let them cloud his head, could not let his human instincts interfere. It had been especially difficult with Marie because she was an absolute animal in bed. While he himself loved to feel a sense of control in all things, Marie had taken things to a different level in the bedroom, switching from the dominator to the slave in the blink of an eye—and being extremely good in both roles. That was why, in the end, he couldn't help but play with her a bit. She liked to be in control most of the time in the bedroom, so he'd had to make her see where she truly fit before he dispatched her. Hanging her in the closet and watching her beg for her life had brought him more pleasure than he would have ever expected.

It was the sole reason he thought he might indeed be capable of murder even after this fourth and final woman was silenced.

It was this thought that crowded his mind as he settled in for sleep. He thought of a future where, once this fourth woman was disposed of, he would experiment with such things. The utter debacle of the police and FBI's handling of the current case was evidence that he could get away with it.

And God, it was enticing.

He fell asleep, wondering what sort of victims he might take in the future and how many different ways he could exert control over them.

It made for a surprisingly dreamless sleep.

***

He was remarkably calm as he drove to his secondary apartment the following morning. When he had first dabbled in sleeping with younger women several years ago, he had rented out the space. Some of the women had boyfriends or fiancés or, in one case, even a husband. And he had his reputation and career to consider.

So a secret secondary living space had just made sense. He'd used it without any problem at all for more than three years, taking nine different women to the apartment for somewhere close to fifty visits. So when he parked his car—his older Subaru, which did not stick out like a sore thumb in this neighborhood like his Beamer—behind the apartment building, it truly did feel like he was at a home away from home.

And there she was, waiting for him. Bridgette Minkus. Twenty-one years old. Pretty in a plain way and she knew it—which was why she was always so eager to please men. She was a firecracker in bed and while she had a few too many restrictions while between the sheets, she made up for it in energy and vigor.

She was in her car, parked two spaces over. Bridgette knew his situation, knew that he had to remain private and, as such, was always in a hurry during these special times. So she played the part, not even saying hello to him as she left her car and walked to the rear entrance of the apartment building. They gave one another a brief and knowing smile as he opened the door for her.

A growing excitement started to spread through him as they made their way through the lobby. As they had practiced in the past, they separated so no one that spotted them would assume they were together. Bridgette took the elevator and he took the stairs. As always, she got there before him; when he came to the top of the stairs, she was already waiting by the door. That excitement in him spiked—and with good reason. He had always gotten excited when he came to this apartment. He'd only ever used it for this one purpose...well, not for what he *currently* had in mind. But to be with women who had few limitations on what they wouldn't do to achieve some level of power. That, he assumed, would excite any man.

But there was a different sort of excitement stirring in him now. The same sort of twisted pleasure that had arisen in him when, as a twelve-year-old boy, he would spy on the teenage girl next door, peering through her window at night while she had sex with her boyfriend.

But this feeling was even more intense, more piercing. The knowledge that Bridgette thought she was going to have a quick romp between classes…the knowledge that he, in fact, intended to kill her.

But the more he thought about it, maybe she'd meet the same fate as Marie. He'd enjoyed the bondage part more than he'd expected. The sense of power and control that came with watching her come to, realizing she had been fooled and was in mortal danger—that was better than any sexual encounter he'd ever had. And he looked forward to experiencing it again.

He unlocked the door. Even as he turned the knob and opened it, her hands were on him. She was pushing him at the back, urging him inside. He wondered if this was because she so badly wanted him or if it was because she was in a hurry to get back to campus for her next class.

He honestly didn't care. When the door shut behind them, he turned to her and pushed her hard against the wall. Bridgette looked surprised, maybe even slightly hurt, but a smile touched the corners of her mouth.

"Since when were you ever rough?" she asked.

She placed her right hand to the side of his face and pulled him close. She kissed him fiercely and he felt no real want in it. No, she was just in a hurry today. He clenched his free hand and, after enduring another five seconds of her kiss, balled that hand into a fist and punched her hard in the chest.

There was more give than he expected and the breath came whooshing out of her in a nearly comical way. The look of pain and surprise on her face enticed him further and he was helpless but to do it again. When he hit her this time, she started to crumple to the floor but he stopped her by grabbing her neck. He throttled her against the wall, shaking her and realizing that he was so hard now it was nearly painful.

Maybe it would be more than tying her up this time. Maybe, like Jo, he'd have her before he got on to the other things.

He literally had to bite back a laugh. So many decisions, all of which he was more than happy to make. He had nowhere to be for several hours and he was going to make very good use of each second he had with her.

As he applied more pressure to her neck and her eyes started to roll back in her head, there was a small flutter of thought somewhere in the back of his head, like a bat coming out of a cave and then turning around instantly to go back inside. That flutter was a distant voice of reason, some long-ago part of him that asked if he was sure this was what he wanted to do…if he was sure this was what he wanted to become.

He'd thought of this at least a dozen times since he strangled Jo Haley…since the idea had come to him the day before he'd killed her. The fact of the matter was that no, he wasn't quite sure.

But if the thrumming energy in his heart and the wild excitement in every muscle in his body was any indication as he started to drag Brigette's body across the apartment, he thought it was far too late to change.

CHAPTER TWENTY THREE

"Mac...you can't just take things from the apartment of a murder victim. I really wish I didn't have to tell you that."

Ellington had taken her news of visiting Christine Lynch's apartment as well as she had expected. He looked upset but also a little excited as he drove them back toward DC.

"I know," she said.

"Are you sure? Because given that you weren't even supposed to be there, I doubt we could use it as evidence."

She could sense his disappointment with her and for that, she truly felt as if she had failed him. On the other hand, Ellington knew that she was not the type who could just move aside and let others do all of the work.

Besides, he was also juggling some new information he had discovered during his morning investigations. Chief among them was the fact that Bruce Dumfries was currently in Washington, DC, meeting with several different non-profit organizations, as well as a few heads of a legislative committee, in preparation for a conference the following day.

Because of this bit of news, Ellington had seemed to not care too much about the pin. The entire confrontation did not escalate into what Mackenzie would have called a fight, but it did create a heavy tension between them. Things were so tense when they returned to their apartment that it was almost a relief when Ellington left to report to McGrath. She knew that there would eventually be hell to pay for keeping the pregnancy from McGrath but for now, he seemed to be at least *somewhat* understanding. She felt a pang of sorrow for Ellington, aware that he was going to have to lie on her behalf about what she had been doing ever since being discharged from the hospital...and that was certainly not how she wanted to start out their marriage.

She fixed herself a small late lunch and sat at the bar, staring at the golden pin she had taken from Christine's apartment. She tried to imagine the excitement of a political fan being invited backstage at a fundraising event. She wondered how many others there had been—how many other women had this same pin.

I wonder if there was a guest list or a list of those invited, she thought. *If we can find that, we might be able to see if there are more targets. We might be able to find out who the killer is going for next.*

Of course, to get that kind of information, she'd have to be assigned to the case. She wondered if Ellington would be willing to reach out to Yardley and Harrison about such a thing.

In the meantime, she could do some digging herself. She knew that if she could find something compelling enough, Ellington would always go to bat for her. So once again, she got behind a laptop—this time using Ellington's old model since hers was currently broken from the scuffle in her hotel room. She was starting to feel like one of those research geeks that used the internet to drum up conspiracies or dirt on famous people—notably celebrities.

She started by looking into Neil Rooney, mainly because his name was so closely linked to everyone they had looked at so far. He was the clearest and most obvious link between the victims. But try as she might, she could not find a single negative thing said about him other than a few snarky Reddit threads. She noted, too, that in a few of those threads, many people were quick to point out that Rooney's campaign manager apparently paid off a woman to shut up about him having raped her and a friend.

She tried to apply her profile to the squeaky clean Rooney. She watched a few YouTube clips of him, including one where he visited a destitute family in Mexico. Even when the man laid into his opponents or those on the far right or left sides of the aisle, he did it with class and dignity. He never slung mud, he never threw people under the bus.

Mackenzie hated to rule people out in such things but she found it very hard to believe that the man she was reading about and watching on YouTube was capable of killing someone...much less strangling them.

She then turned her attention to where she really didn't want it to go. She'd heard horror stories of agents with both the FBI and the CIA who had lost their jobs because they had gone looking in the wrong places when it came to US politics. And while someone like Bruce Dumfries wielded no real power of his own, she knew there would be powerful people he was connected through thanks to the all-powerful thread of money.

She felt the weight of her decision the moment she typed the name *Bruce Dumfries* into the Google search bar. She was about to jump down a rabbit hole she had no business diving into. Even if she were actively on the case, she'd have some hesitation about looking into a lobbyist. Lobbyists tended to have links and connections that were buried deep, far beyond the public eye, no matter how good their intentions may be.

As she started to look into Dumfries, Mackenzie began to realize that all she truly knew about the man that he was a lobbyist. And that was about it.

She soon discovered Dumfries had a criminal history that came up quite quickly on her web search. He'd been arrested for drug possession in the '80s and for a disturbing the peace complaint in the early '90s during a protest outside of the Pentagon where he had been involved in a melee that ended up breaking a woman's nose. When he was called out for hitting a woman, he was literally degraded by the media and massively ridiculed. However, when a video of the event made the news, it was revealed that it was not Dumfries who had punched the woman. Rather than boast that he had been right all along, he let it slide and faded into obscurity. After that, he was known for making generous donations to Planned Parenthood and several different environmental programs.

And that's where the trail on Bruce Dumfries seemed to die down. She did find easy connections to him and the Rooney campaign, though his name was never explicitly linked to Daniel Humphrey's.

She did find one mention of Dumfries in direct correlation with Eric Connor, though. Several years ago, one of Connor's bodyguards quit unexpectedly. In the single interview she could find with the bodyguard, he stated that the relationship he had with Connor was just fine—it was the some of the people he had associated with.

Namely, Bruce Dumfries.

***

When Ellington arrived home, Mackenzie wasted no time. She felt that if she didn't tell him right away, the anticipation and worry of it would make her sick to her stomach—not something she wanted to experience while also growing a human being in there.

To his credit, Ellington handled it well. He did not interrupt her as she told him how she had spent her afternoon. He listened to her for a full six minutes as she filled him in and showed him some of the online content she had found. She had the article about the bodyguard pulled up, ready for him to read if he chose to do so.

"He's not specific at all," she said. "He just says there were people that Connor was associating with that he did not agree with. He said sometimes it made for a tense and stressful work environment—added pressure you didn't really look for when it came to being a bodyguard for a politician."

When she was finally done explaining her train of thought, he was sitting on the couch, leaning back and looking at her as if he was trying to see through her.

"Mac," he said. "It all sounds really promising. But if Dumfries was indeed linked to Eric Connor so directly...you don't go after someone like that unless you are absolutely positive."

"You don't think I know that?" she asked. "I've been debating on it for the last hour and a half. But if I didn't at least pursue it and this killer is never found, I'd always wonder. It would haunt me."

"Besides...we've been digging up stuff on him all day," Ellington said. "We found exactly the same things you did. The good news is that we know he's in DC."

"You said he's going to be at that conference tomorrow, right? I think Rooney is scheduled to speak, too."

"That's right. So if we do indeed need to get to Dumfries, he's right here in our own backyard."

"Did you find the name of the bodyguard? The article never mentions it."

"We did," he said, the tone in his voice indicating that he did not like where this was headed.

"We just need to speak with him," Mackenzie said. "Even if he can't provide enough evidence to go after Bruce Dumfries, he's sure to know *something* about the darker dealings within that group."

"And why do you think there are dark dealings at all?"

"All of the victims were behind the scenes of the campaign with these men. Politicians. I hate to paint them all with a wide brush but...three dead women, all connected to powerful men. Even if Humphrey or Dumfries turns out to be innocent, maybe this bodyguard knows about enemies they would have had. Maybe he knows deeper details about enemies Rooney or Eric Connor have made along the way. There's a whole pool of potential suspects in what he might be able to tell us."

He nodded and she could tell that he was doing his best to think like she did. He was trying to think of her not as his wife and the soon-to-be mother of his child. He was seeing her as the gifted special agent now, reminding himself how instinctual she could be.

"I've thought the same thing," he said. "It might seem like a long shot, but it's certainly worth looking into. If we don't have a suspect soon, and if Dumfries does indeed check out, we'd probably have to go to the bodyguard anyway."

"Does he live in DC?" she asked.

"No. Richmond. Intel suggests that once he quit his job, he moved to Richmond, Virginia, to take care of his ailing mother."

"We can go first thing in the morning, right?"

"We?"

She hated to come off like a bitch, but she could not just sit by on this. After all, they were just paying the man a visit. There was no danger involved.

"Yes. *We*."

"McGrath would kill both of us."

"Then we don't tell him. I'm…God. This sounds so terrible. But I'm not going to be active anymore after this. Just let me tag along and be there when you question him. You take the lead. I'll just be there."

"My arm candy," he said with a smile. "I guess if we're married, I need to get used to that."

She walked over to him and kissed him softly and playfully on the lips. "Thank you."

"Don't thank me yet. You have to know…even if we find anything of value, we're talking about going after a lobbyist that is tightly linked to a senator. Even if Eric Connor has no idea about the vile shit this guy might be doing…it affects him, too."

"I know."

As she said that, another thing suddenly dawned on her. The men who had accosted her in the hotel room…to have been sent by someone as small-time as Daniel Humphrey just didn't make sense. It made her wonder if a man like Dumfries—a man who was used to tossing money at things he believed in or wanted to see pushed through—he would probably do the same to eliminate something that was standing in his way.

"I think we *do* need to talk about this," Ellington said.

"About what?"

He took a moment to answer, choosing his words carefully. "Your inability to just let things go. I saw it first with the case concerning your father. And I love that about you—the drive and the determination. But you don't always have to be the one saving people, you know? You don't always have to shoulder that burden. Sometimes it's perfectly okay to allow others to help."

The comment stung a bit, but she knew he was right. And honestly, she thought she might have been able to completely release this current case if it hadn't been for the two men who had attacked her; they had not only put her own life in jeopardy, but her child's as well.

For her, that was more than enough reason to stay attached to the case in any way possible.

No matter the cost.

CHAPTER TWENTY FOUR

They were on the road the following morning, headed out of DC toward Richmond at seven o'clock to meet with a man named Earl Jackson, former bodyguard of Eric Connor. Mackenzie could tell that Ellington was on edge, probably feeling both guilty and scared for his job due to her accompanying him.

"I could have stayed at home," she said when they were about halfway through the trip.

"You and I both know that's a lie. Even if I had have managed to leave without you, I would have not heard the end of it for a very long time. Or you would have given me the silent treatment."

"I don't do the silent treatment."

"Whatever the case…we both know there was no way in hell you would have let me speak to Jackson without you coming along."

"You're right," she said. "I was just trying to be a sweet and accommodating wife."

"For the record, I would have *preferred* you stay at home."

"Noted."

"I'm serious. We're not just talking about your safety anymore. This isn't even about the baby. This is your *job*. I remember that detective I met a few years back in Nebraska. I remember how trapped she felt. I saw then that you were meant for better things. And you worked your ass off to get those things. I don't want to see you lose it all just because you can't let things go."

Again, she felt as if he was attacking her. But she also knew he was only saying these things because he genuinely cared for her and wanted the best for her. It was this that allowed her to push the slight hurt to the side and reach out for his hand.

She looked through the windshield and enjoyed the silence that fell in around them. She was coming to understand that when two people were in love and relying on one another for just about everything, even uncomfortable silences delivered quite a bit of peace.

***

Earl Jackson actually lived a bit outside of Richmond, beyond the Short Pump area. They pulled into his driveway just shy of nine a.m., right behind a large black Ford pickup truck. He had a nice home, a two-story brick house along a cul de sac in a wealthy neighborhood. The neighborhood was quiet as they walked to the door and knocked, the only commotion coming from an elderly man walking his dog just a bit up the sidewalk.

Several seconds later, the door was answered by a tall bald man. He was wearing a Navy T-shirt and a pair of jeans. He carried a cup of coffee in one hand and had the look of a man who was preoccupied with something.

"Can I help you?" he asked.

"Are you Mr. Earl Jackson?" Ellington asked.

"Who's asking?"

Ellington was the only one to show his badge. He was once more taking the lead, making sure Mackenzie did not insert herself in any significant way unless she had to. "I'm Agent Ellington and this is my partner, Agent White."

She saw the traces of a smile touch the corner of his mouth as he referred to her in such a way. Apparently, they were both having trouble getting used to her new name.

Earl Jackson looked a little frightened. His posture seemed to spread out a bit, as if he would block the doorway into his home if he had to.

"What's this about?" he asked.

"We're working on an investigation in Maryland that brought up a few different names from people that are involved in the government. One of those people just happened to be a lobbyist by the name of Bruce Dumfries. A man we know you disliked enough to quit a job and sever ties with Senator Eric Connor. We were hoping to speak to you about how you knew him."

"Yeah. I'm not interested in that," Jackson said.

"I can respect that," Ellington said. "But this is a very pressing investigation and we need information that isn't exactly readily available."

Jackson eyed them skeptically and sipped from his coffee. "What sort of investigation?"

"We think there might be some men around Dumfries and Connor that could potentially know some details about a murder case we are trying to solve."

Mackenzie noted right away that Ellington had not inferred that they were eyeing Dumfries for the murder. It was a smart move, not giving Jackson the ability to automatically see the man in a new negative light.

That look of fear came back into Jackson's eyes. Without his saying a word, the expression spoke volumes. Jackson stepped aside and nodded for them to come in. "My wife is at work. If she were here, there might be some push-back on me allowing this."

"Can we ask why?" Mackenzie asked as they stepped inside.

"Well, I assume you're here because you know I once worked for Eric. And, as you said, that I quit. Well, things didn't end there. I was relentlessly harassed by that asshole after I quit."

"Dumfries being the asshole?" Ellington asked.

"Yes."

"And why did he harass you?"

"He claimed I said too much when I left my position with Eric. Said I tossed him under the bus. Which is stupid. I had two people interview me. One of those, I shut down about a minute into it and revealed nothing. And the second one, I did my best to say it was because I felt uncomfortable working in such a position when he was around. And that was it."

"What do you mean by *harassed*?" Ellington said.

They were in the living room now, Jackson taking a seat in a recliner. Ellington sat down on a couch opposite the recliner while Mackenzie remained standing next to him. It was a comfy place that seemed to draw the tension right out of all three of them.

"Well, I originally moved to Richmond because my mother was in a convalescent home. She passed away about two months after I moved here. But by that time, my wife had picked up a really good job so we stayed. I work from home, helping remotely set up security systems for growing businesses, so I can work anywhere. So we just stayed here. We would get phone calls from people that used to work for Eric, threatening us. I called Eric and told him and it stopped for a while. But then there was one time where Dumfries himself showed up at our old home in downtown Richmond. He had a goon with him that constantly kept reaching for his waist, like he was packing heat."

"Were there ever any physical altercations?" Ellington asked.

"No. Look...to be honest, the only reason I ever said anything about my reasons for quitting is because I figured it would become public record. If I ended up missing or dead, I figured that one little statement I made would instantly have people looking in Bruce Dumfries's direction."

"That raises a ton of questions," Ellington said. "For starters, what was the relationship between Dumfries and Connor?"

"Oh, they were thick as thieves. Best friends. They disagreed on a lot of things, but they always had each other's back. You see, Dumfries came from money. Old money. His family has been loaded ever since the early 1900s. When his father passed away and most of that money went to an already wealthy Bruce Dumfries, he ended up being worth around two hundred and sixty million dollars. And as I'm sure you know, he sprinkles it around Washington, earning favors and making powerful friends. One of those friends was Eric Connor."

"Any problems with Connor?"

"Not at all. That man was great to me. Treated me well. A real stand-up guy. Which is why it blows my mind that he was friends with Dumfries…why he always covered up for the creep."

"Covered up what, exactly?"

"All sorts of sordid shit. My partner and I would get calls when we were working for Eric…calls from Eric himself. He would ask us to go to the Dumfries residence and, as Eric would phrase it, *clean up the mess.* Turns out, Dumfries was a fan of beating his wife almost weekly. Cleaning up the mess was making sure she didn't tell anyone. Paying her off, talking her down. Sometimes it was making sure she didn't need to go to the hospital."

"And was she ever seriously hurt?" Mackenzie asked.

"He snapped her wrist once. Broke her nose, too."

"He was married twice, correct?" Ellington asked.

"Yeah."

"What about the second wife?"

"Dumfries and his second wife stopped living together after about a week. But he begged her to stay with him, just out of public image interest. She did, and they stayed together for about a year. He cheated on her constantly. We'd get calls about that, too. Calls to check on the prostitutes and escorts Dumfries had hired. He knocked a few teeth out, nearly strangled one. But he paid them off for their silence."

Mackenzie and Ellington shared a look at this news. "And why did you not share all of this when you stepped out?"

"Because he's bad news." He left it at this for a moment. Mackenzie thought he was starting to grow uncomfortable again, maybe regretting everything he'd said. "I don't know it for sure, but I'm pretty sure Dumfries had at least two people killed while I was working for Eric. And I *know* he regularly made threats to people. He was very intimidating. But he was charming in the public eye so when he showed this dark side of his behind closed doors, it was almost paralyzing. He's very good at showing the world one face while saving the other for just a select few. It also helped that he plays the innocence card—always trying to stay out of the spotlight. But when it does hit him, he plays it up well."

"What makes you think he had people killed?" Ellington asked.

"There was this online journalist that started to kick up a story. He'd found out about the prostitutes, only when he came after the story, he came for Eric. Had his facts wrong and Eric proved it. So the reporter dug deeper and ended up finding Dumfries was the one he was looking for. He ended up speaking to an old college roommate of Eric's...a guy that knew Dumfries well, too. I think this guy tipped Dumfries off because he ended up requesting a meeting with him. I know this for a fact because Eric had us check the guy out for Dumfries before they met. So the reporter and Dumfries met and then no one saw him for like two days. And when he came back to work, he was quite happy. As for the journalist, he was found three weeks later in a pond somewhere out in the country. He'd been beaten to death with a baseball bat."

"And no one made the connection?" Mackenzie asked.

"One person did. Again...this is all assumptions on my part. Just connecting the dots. But the person that got suspicious and started asking questions after the journalist was found...I know for a fact that a check for thirty thousand dollars was written to her. Straight from one of Eric's accounts so it wouldn't be linked to Dumfries."

"Sounds like Eric Connor wasn't as innocent as he seems, either."

"He dabbled, too. He had two prostitutes he would see regularly. But that was after his marriage ended. As far as I know, he never did that sort of thing when he was married. But his connection with Dumfries...I never got it. Never understood it."

"You're making it sound like with Connor as a shield of sorts, Dumfries is untouchable," Ellington said.

"He might be. He was always good at shoveling over his crap. And when he needed help, Eric was there. Dumfries loves control and he loves power. But he also knows that if he made much of himself, all of his little dark delights would be called out and shown to the world. He's happy to stay where he is. He's comfortable there, shelling out his money from the dark. He's made strong friends and I'm pretty sure he has some low-rate bodyguard around him most of the time. The kind that came to my house with him to threaten me. I'd imagine the same kind that did away with the journalist."

"Mr. Jackson...do you have any proof of any of this?"

"Nothing tangible. But I received calls from Eric…calls where he told us that there was another mess at the Dumfries house that needed to be taken care of. I only ever actually spoke to Dumfries on a few occasions. I hated him. I felt like he saw me as his clean-up crew, a little peon that worked for him as well as for Eric."

"What about the other bodyguard that was working with you at the time?" Ellington asked. "Could he corroborate these stories?"

"I'm sure he'd love to, but he can't. Not too long after I left, he left, too. He told no one where he went and left no trace. I've often wondered if he'd also had enough but maybe Dumfries got to him before he could escape."

"So if we tried getting a meeting with Dumfries…"

"I'd be careful," Jackson said. "FBI or not…the man has some weird and powerful ties. I still don't quite know how. There's a rumor floating around that he was very good friends with Richard King back in college."

"Richard King," Ellington said. "You mean the head of the Justice Department?"

"That's him. Also…he'll have people fighting for him. When Eric was reelected the last term, it was a close election. His winning tipped the senate and he made it known that a lot of his success came from loyal friends and supporters like Dumfries. He actually called the fucker out in his victory speech, thanking him. If Dumfries goes down, Eric would be affected, too. Control of the senate would basically be up for grabs. And Maryland needed that win…the Democratic party did, anyway. There's too much at stake."

"Mr. Jackson," Ellington said. "Do you have a number for how many women he abused?"

Jackson shook his head. "No. I know there were at least two. Three if you count his first wife."

"Do you know where his first wife is now?"

"No idea. I intentionally never really tried to keep up with him."

"Any idea how long it's been since you received one of those threatening visits or phone calls?" Mackenzie asked.

"It's been over a year. That's why I was hesitant to let you in. It's been a year and I was daring to hope that chapter of my life was finally over." He stopped here and looked directly at Ellington. "Look… if you go after him, it has to be a certain and ironclad thing. It has to be in a way where he doesn't have a chance to set his goons on you or to pay to have what you find covered up. And while I hate to think of Eric in such a way, I think Dumfries could sway him. And if he gets Eric on you, the bureau would get hit with so much crap…"

"Trust me," Ellington said. "We'll take every precaution."

Jackson nodded, but didn't seem too convinced. "I wish you the best of luck. I know I'd sleep a lot easier at night if that son of a bitch was finally taken down."

"You talk about him like he's some kind of monster," Ellington said.

Jackson shrugged and asked: "Jekyll and Hyde…was that guy a monster?"

"No," Mackenzie said. "Just a doctor that had an evil side that came out."

"That's Dumfries, then. That's him exactly."

He ended this statement with a look that sent a little chill through Mackenzie. It was the look of a man that knew the monster—and also knew that as long as monsters had shadows to lurk around it, they would always exist.

CHAPTER TWENTY FIVE

"Agent White, how have you been?"

It was a loaded question, particularly coming from McGrath, through the other end of her phone. She looked out of the windshield, the next exit for DC coming up. They'd left Earl Jackson behind an hour and a half ago and she was still fighting the chills from that encounter. When she had seen the call from McGrath coming through, the chill increased but she knew it would be useless to ignore the call.

"I'm good," she answered. "Maybe a little out of sorts."

"Rested, I hope? Your head doing better?"

"Yes sir. You got the medical reports yet?"

"No. They'll be here soon. Look...Mackenzie..."

A flash of warmth passed through her—whether from fear or actual emotion, she wasn't sure; McGrath had never referred to her by her first name.

"I've been thinking more and more about it, and I feel that I know you well enough to understand why you chose not to let me know about the pregnancy right away," he continued. "But at the same time, I consider it reckless for you to have been in such an active capacity these last few days. It makes me feel truly terrible to think that something could have happened to the baby just because you opted to not tell me about it. It's made me realize that I value you more than I probably show."

"Thank you, sir."

"I want you to take the remainder of the week off," he said. "But I want to schedule a meeting with you on Monday morning. Nine o'clock, in my office. I want to go over some options about how to keep you on cases without you feeling the need to play Wonder Woman. And we also need to go over maternity leave and all of that."

"Yes sir. I appreciate that."

"Enjoy the next few days. I won't lie...you probably have some desk-riding in the future. But I'm sure you'll excel at whatever I put in front of you. Take care, Agent White. Or is it Ellington now?"

"We're still dancing around that one," she said.

They ended the call and Mackenzie honestly wasn't sure how to feel. Here they were, actively going against McGrath's orders for her to stay off her feet, when he had called to deliver what was easily the most touching sentiment she had ever seen from him. It made her feel awful.

"That was McGrath?" Ellington asked.

"Yeah. It was sort of touching."

She dwelled on the conversation for a moment and realized that perhaps one of the reasons she was finding it so hard to take a back seat on this case was because it had come about during a time of huge transition. She had been married, she was going to have a child, and, beyond all of that, her career seemed to be on a great trajectory. The fact that McGrath hadn't just chewed her ass out was proof of that.

And honestly, why ruin a transition with feeling like she had failed in bringing a case to a close? Why kill her momentum in such a way?

She looked back out to the road, thinking over one more detail she had picked up yesterday. She had mentioned it to Ellington but almost in passing, as if it weren't all that important.

It was the fact that Bruce Dumfries would not be speaking at the conference tomorrow, but Senator Connor would be. So that, at least, made it clear why Dumfries would be there.

And the venue was only four hours away from their apartment.

It certainly had her thinking, even after the heartfelt call from McGrath.

"You okay?" Ellington asked.

"Yeah," she said, hoping it wasn't obvious that her mind was preoccupied. "Just thinking."

***

Later that afternoon, Ellington was called back in to headquarters to hop on a conference call with Yardley, Harrison, and the bureau resource department. He'd received a call and a few emails concerning the case, all of which he shared with Mackenzie before he left.

For starters, Yardley and Harrison got a positive ID on the man who had been in the hotel lobby, asking for Mackenzie. He had seemed to be aware of where the cameras were, always lowering his face when he was within range of one. But there had been a few frames when he had been speaking to the woman at the desk where his face had come into view. His name was Donnie Curts and he had a pretty extensive criminal record which included breaking and entering as well as a few months in prison for fracturing a man's arm during a home invasion. A manhunt was currently underway to find him.

In other news, Daniel Humphrey had decided to sic his lawyer on the bureau, a tactic that looked like it was going to blow up in his face since he was the one who looked like the bad guy in the entire thing.

"And here's the real kicker," Ellington had said as he'd started to make his way for the door. "Neil Rooney is scheduled to make some sort of an announcement this afternoon. Rumors are swirling that say it's a statement to inform the public that he will no longer allow Humphrey as his campaign manager."

It made Mackenzie feel slightly blind; maybe even a little naïve. They'd spent so much time focusing on the man at the lower end of the totem pole that they had neglected to look up. After hearing about the alleged crimes and twisted behavior of Bruce Dumfries, the skeletons that Humphrey had been dancing with seemed innocent by comparison.

Ellington was at the door by then and Mackenzie realized that she was following behind him closely, like the dutiful little wife seeing her husband off to work. She stopped in her tracks when this feeling came over her and they shared a kiss before he left.

Mackenzie walked to the living room and sat down hard on the couch. If this was what she had to expect in the final months of her pregnancy and the weeks following delivery, she was not looking forward to it. She was an introvert at heart, yes, but she also could not handle sitting still. Especially not when there was a case at her feet that had not yet been solved.

She wasted no time in pretending that she was going to be able to ignore the fact that Dumfries would be making a very public appearance at a conference tomorrow. She grabbed the laptop and pulled up information on the conference. She quickly realized that calling it a conference was really just a polite formality. What it really was in disguise was a fundraiser for several different Democratic groups—which Mackenzie had no problem with. But when she saw wording about the real intention in small print near the bottom of the pages, as well as a schedule filled with speakers like Eric Connor and Neil Rooney, she couldn't help but roll her eyes. It might be painted as a conference, but it was really just an excuse for men and women of power to stand up in front of those who had elected them, reminding them that thanks to the public's votes, they were in control.

Control...power...sounds like the perfect place for a man like Dumfries.

But another thought came on the heels of this. One that hurt but also pissed her off.

This is the type of thing you need to share with your husband...not as your bureau partner, but as the man you're now married to—the man that will be the father of your child.

She was starting to hatch a plan. She had a good idea of what she needed to do. The only question left was whether or not she would include Ellington. Her husband. A man who was supposed to trust her and, at the same time, unequivocally always be there for her.

Exactly, she thought. *What sort of example are you setting to start your marriage by hiding something like this from him? If you go through with your little plan, he's going to find out anyway.*

She felt selfish but she also felt dignified. As her husband, she thought he would understand. Maybe he'd even support her in it.

Done reading about the conference, Mackenzie shut down the browser and closed the laptop. She sat still on the couch and stared into space, thinking long and hard about it for a very long time.

***

It was becoming almost like a routine now, and Mackenzie was acutely aware that it was not how a marriage should start out. Ellington came home at 7:30 that evening and he hadn't even had a chance to fully come inside and take off his coat before she came clean with him, telling her what she had planned.

He paused for only a moment, giving her a crooked smile and a sigh of frustration. He shrugged his coat off, hung it in the coat closet, and turned to her. He looked at her in the same way he had looked at her so many times during their trip to Iceland—a trip that even now, just four days after having left, seemed like it occurred ages ago.

"Mackenzie, I love you very much," he said. "But are you out of your fucking mind?"

"It feels right," Mackenzie said.

"Maybe it does. And it certainly does seem to line up with everything we're looking for in a suspect. But this is a whole new ballgame. If I got to McGrath with the suggestion that our killer is a powerful lobbyist that is closely attached to what seems to be a clueless US Senator, you know he's going to demand physical proof. And we just don't have that."

"You're right," she said. She knew this just as well as Ellington did. Which was why she was fully prepared to go it on her own. The plan she had in mind was one of minimal risk, one she thought Ellington might get on board with.

"I just want you to hear me out. I've got a plan and—"

"You usually do," he said with a smile.

That smile told her everything she needed to know about the future of their marriage. In Ellington, she was going to have a husband who would always hear her out, a husband who would never shoot an idea down right away. He would always be in her corner and even if he disagreed with her, he would always hear her out.

He did that then and there, in that moment. He listened to her as she walked him through the plan she had set up in her mind. She explained it very carefully, not wanting to miss a single detail. She knew that she was asking a lot of him—to do something a bit controversial behind McGrath's back. But the risk was worth the potential gain. And even before she was done explaining what she had on mind, she could tell that Ellington felt the same way.

And when she reached the end, he was nodding. The look of anxiousness on his face told her everything she needed to know. If she had any doubts, he said one single sentence that confirmed it for her.

With a heavy sigh of resignation, he took her hand and said: "Okay...let's do it."

CHAPTER TWENTY SIX

The conference was being held at the Capital View Conference Center. When Mackenzie and Ellington arrived there the following day, the conference itself started to make more sense to Mackenzie. There were big name speakers, of course—from Eric Connor, Neil Rooney, and even the current press secretary. After the main speakers were done, there were other, much smaller and lesser known figures, who were holding Q and As and even workshops on how to bolster interest in voting, international relations, and politics in general.

When Mackenzie picked up one of the programs as they walked into the conference center, she saw that Eric Connor was hosting one of the smaller break-off sessions.

She also saw something else she had seen on the website yesterday. The morning would start off with small speeches from the key speakers: a local musician who had just signed a major record deal and was currently making the transition to a political advocate, Neil Rooney, and then Eric Connor. They would be speaking in that order, meaning that sometime before ten a.m., Mackenzie would have the opportunity to carry out her plan.

Directly beyond the small welcome center where she had picked up the program, there was a small security station. The attendees were being asked to file in through three different lanes, passing by guards with metal-detecting wands. As they filed into one of the lines, Mackenzie watched as people placed their loose change, cell phones, and other miscellaneous metallic items into small trays that were then passed behind the guards by another guard and given back to their owners.

Ellington was in front of Mackenzie and when he reached the guard in their line, he quickly and very subtly flashed his FBI ID. Mackenzie did the same and they also both quickly pulled their jackets aside to show their sidearms. The guard gave a quick nod and ushered them through, drawing no attention to any of it.

"I want to stress just one more time," Ellington said, "just how much of a bad idea I think this is."

"You said it was a good idea last night."

"Well, the *idea* is good. And so is the conceptualization. I'm talking more along the lines of my pregnant wife taking part in it. And not letting our direct supervisor know what we're up to."

Mackenzie wasn't going to argue the point, so she said nothing. They made their way through the central lobby and entered the auditorium in the back of the building. It was a decent-sized space, seating around seven hundred or so. There was very light music playing, something upbeat and instrumental. The place was well lit as a few stagehands made some last-minute adjustments at the stage.

Most of the seats down front were already filled, so Mackenzie and Ellington had to settle with seats along the fifth row from the stage. When she was seated, Mackenzie studied the place, making a map of possible outcomes in her head. She was quite certain the speakers would come out from the doorway in the back, behind the slightly risen stage and to the right. They'd likely exit that way as well. In terms of exits, there was a single door to the left, about halfway along the floor where all of the attendees would be seated. Other than that, there were the two sets of double doors they had come through.

She assumed Dumfries would be sitting very close to the stage, or maybe even just hanging back behind the stage. In other words, getting up close and personal with him was going to be tougher than she thought. Habitually, she reached into the inner pocket of her jacket, feeling the shape of her phone—hopefully the only weapon she'd be needing to use today.

"You nervous?" Ellington asked.

"No."

It was a lie. Her nerves were all over the place, which was not like her. Maybe that was because she knew exactly what was at stake. It could go one of two ways this morning: she'd leave here with enough evidence to file an official investigation and potentially have Dumfries arrested, or she'd leave empty-handed. It was an all or nothing situation that she truly started to feel the weight of as more and more people filed into the auditorium.

Fifteen minutes later, the conference officially began. The event emcee came out and ran through a list of the day's schedule and then introduced the first guest, the local politically motivated musician. Mackenzie had never heard of him and, therefore, found it easy to tune out and amp herself up for the next half an hour or so.

The musician spoke for about twenty minutes and left the stage to a respectable amount of applause. The emcee came back out and introduced the next speaker. When the name "Neil Rooney" came out of his mouth, Mackenzie tensed up a bit. She watched Rooney come out to thunderous applause. He was a good-looking man in his late thirties and he knew how to work a crowd exceptionally well. His speech was short and sweet, extoling the importance of voting and the ability for both parties to reach across the aisle for the betterment of the country. He was off of the stage twelve minutes later, leaving the crowd cheering.

No more than thirty seconds passed before the emcee came back out. He ran down the list of events for the afternoon and then transitioned into the introduction for the next speaker. When he introduced Eric Connor, there wasn't quite as big of a reception as there had been for Rooney, but it was still impressive.

Mackenzie found herself instantly looking down around at the audience. She'd seen a few pictures of Humphries online and he looked quite plain in all of them. Still, she thought she would recognize him in this crowd.

Connor took a few moments to let the applause wash over him for a few moments while he waved and smiled to the crowd. Right away, she could see the charm in the man—from his smile to the way he carried himself. He was fifty-two and he could easily pass as forty. He had an almost Kennedy-like quality to him with just an edge of moodiness.

When he spoke, his voice was soft but firm. He articulated each and every word and it was clear for his posture, stature, and ease that he knew how to work a crowd. Mackenzie listened to him as much as she could, thinking of how Earl Jackson had seemed so baffled and sad that Connor could keep company like Dumfries.

On the stage, Connor spoke about making sure minorities were treated better in the next election and how the well-to-do could play their part in making that happen. He also spoke about how DC had a very negative stereotype when it came to getting things done—a stereotype he believed was a fair one but, with the help of voters and elected officials who actually gave a damn, could be changed in the course of a single election cycle.

His speech went on for about half an hour as he gave examples of unprecedented voter turnouts in some of the county's poorest areas. And he had to stop about every two or three minutes for applause breaks. The man knew what he was doing and she saw right away that if he wanted, he could easily have a much better career if he shot for larger elected offices. Of course, she remembered what Earl Jackson had said about Dumfries—how he preferred the shadows. She wondered if the same was true of

Connor. Was he perfectly happy with his role as a Senator, or did he have bigger office-related goals?

As his tone shifted and he ramped down a bit, Mackenzie could tell when his talk was wrapping up. Earlier, she had watched the emcee coming in and exiting from the door along the back behind the stage. As she tried to figure out a way to meet with Connor face to face—assuming that would be her best bet to confront Dumfries—he said something from the stage that she couldn't quite believe…something that might make her plan infinitely simpler.

"I've been told that we'll be having a little intermission once I stop running my mouth," he said with a chuckle. "About twenty minutes or so. During that time, I'll be out in the lobby that you all entered through if anyone has questions or comments for me. I hope to see some of you out there!"

With that, Eric Connor left the stage and, just like the emcee and the musician before him, he made his exit through the door behind the stage. Ellington nudged Mackenzie and gave her a *can you believe this* look. He looked excited, clearly feeling the same relief she was feeling.

"Might as well be the first ones there to greet him," Mackenzie said, already getting to her feet. But she didn't give Connor any attention. She was too busy looking for Dumfries.

And there he was. In the front row, getting up and heading to the right. He said something to a member of the security team, was allowed to the side of the stage, and then followed a few seconds behind Connor.

Mackenzie and Ellington quickly got out of their seats and headed for the aisle that ran along the center of the room, between the two separate sections of seating. Others were already doing the same ahead of them but because they moved fast, Mackenzie felt that they wouldn't have much of a wait. Just to be prepared, she went ahead and enacted the first part of her plan; she took her cell phone out of her pocket, opened up the voice recording app, and placed it back into her pocket with the app still running.

As they neared the double doors that headed out to the lobby, Mackenzie took note of a man up by the rear wall. He was slowly approaching the doors and seemed to be looking directly at them. She had noticed a couple of cleverly placed security personnel throughout the morning—which made sense, given the stature of a few of the speakers. And while this man carried himself as such, he simply looked a little out of place.

She was about to comment on this to Ellington as they neared the door but by then, there was no time. The man was at the door just as Ellington was about to pass through.

"Agent?" the man asked, gently placing a hand on Ellington's arm.

Ellington looked at the man's hand, resting on the top of his arm, and said, "Yeah?"

"Could I have a word with you?"

A look of skepticism came over Ellington's face. He shook the man's hand away from his arm and said, "What do you need?"

"Just a word. I believe there might be something you need to hear...something urgent. I'm trying to be as discreet as possible without causing a scene here. It won't take two minutes."

"Who are you?"

"I'm with the security team."

Ellington looked back at Mackenzie and then out into the lobby where a small crowd was already forming as Eric Connor appeared from around the corner.

"It's okay," Mackenzie said. "I'll meet you out there. I'll wait for you before..."

Ellington nodded but still didn't seem very comfortable with the situation. Still, he gave Mackenzie one last glance as he quickly followed the security employee back along the aisle and down toward the stage.

That's odd, Mackenzie thought as she walked through the doorway and into the lobby. *It must be something fairly serious if the security team kept in mind that there were FBI agents in attendance. But why only Ellington?*

Something did indeed seem off about it. She tried to figure out what it was as she joined the crowd. It was still growing, people filing in from the auditorium and from the hallways along the sides. She noted that there were two cameramen in attendance as well, the logos of local news programs on the sides of their cameras. Diligent reporters stood beside them, waiting for Connor to make a brief statement before taking questions from the gathered crowd.

And there was Dumfries, to his right. He wasn't at his right hand, but he was close. Earl Jackson hadn't been kidding about how the two were linked. Something about it seemed a little venomous to Mackenzie...as if there was one there to protect the other, to strike if the other was attacked.

She tried her best to think of how to go about the next step. Her original plan was to go after Connor—to ask about having former employees clean up the messes that his lobbyist friends made. It would be a cheap shot for sure but she knew how men in control worked. If she pushed hard enough, Dumfries would show *something*. She'd seen it numerous times during interrogations and takedowns.

If she had to, she'd drop the name of one of the women she now felt fairly certain were his victims. The look on his face at the mention of the names would likely tell all of the story.

Of course, this is the first man I will have ever accused of something so blatantly that has a very public reputation to uphold, she thought.

Two rows of people were all that separated her from Connor when he gave a very brief introductory speech. "Most of you know how these things go," he said, his tone casual and conversational. "Let's keep it clean, quick, and simple. If you're with the press and require a little more time, I can make some time once the conference kicks back up. Now, which of you fine folks would like to ask the first question?"

The question was on Mackenzie's tongue. She was fully prepared to shout it out over the din of the crowd—a group of people that had now grown to about fifty people or so.

But before she could get the question out, a young man directly in front of Connor asked a question about property taxes. Connor answered. Beside him, separated by only two other people—one of whom she was pretty sure was security in disguise—stood Bruce Dumfries.

Slowly, she stepped forward. She wanted her voice recorder to catch everything that was said.

"Any other questions?" Connor asked.

"Right here," Mackenzie said, raising her hand.

Eric Connor looked her way. So did Dumfries and the security guard. She gauged Dumfries's reaction and…it didn't make sense. He seemed to not care at all. But Eric Connor looked alarmed for a moment. For a split second, there had been recognition on his face…as if he knew her.

She stepped up to the front of the crowd, making sure everyone standing there in attendance could see her. "I was wondering what you might know about the three young ladies from Queen Nash University that were recently murdered."

The scene went absolutely quiet. Dumfries was looking at her now, but he was confused. Connor, on the other hand, went pale and his posture changed right away. It looked as if an electric current had passed through his body. Still, he was quick to answer.

"I know very little about it," he said. "Just what I have read in the papers. And I believe there was a great deal of interest in my former colleague, Daniel Humphrey. Very unfortunate."

Mackenzie felt herself losing her moment. She was taken aback by the sudden development that had played out in front of her. Dumfries had shown no reaction when he saw her, but Connor had. Dumfries had showed only stark confusion when she had mentioned the murders, but Connor had looked mortified for a single moment.

But then she once again thought of Earl Jackson. Something about the journalist that had caught on to Dumfries.

That journalist thought the trouble was coming from Connor at first. Whatever clues and leads the journalist had originally led him to Connor...

"Each one of them had VIP pins from last fall's campaign," Mackenzie added. She then pulled the pin she had gotten from Christine Lynch's apartment out of her pocket and held it up. "Just like this one…taken from the apartment of the second victim."

Cameras flashed and people started to murmur. Meanwhile, Eric Connor looked enraged. In a moment of absolute unawareness, he looked over to Dumfries. Dumfries only shrugged, the color also going out of his face.

Mackenzie stepped forward, now less than a foot away from Connor. The security member beside him stepped forward to cut her off but Mackenzie continued to talk.

"You met them all at a gala event, didn't you?"

"I'm afraid you're mistaken," Connor said. But his voice was shaken and he was clearly rocked. He looked like he might get sick.

It was Connor that Earl Jackson and his bodyguard partner were cleaning up after, Mackenzie realized. *The journalist was right from the start. It was Connor…and Dumfries was just the scapegoat. And he did it, in exchange for some extra power. In exchange for essentially being untouchable.*

"You like hurting women, right?" she asked.

Some people in the crowd started to grumble. The security guard stepped forward, blocking her view of Connor.

"You strangled them, right? Jo Haley, Christine Lynch…"

"That's enough," the security guard said.

"You dumped Marie Totino in the river! What was wrong? Couldn't control her? Couldn't make her—"

Suddenly, Eric Connor sprang forward. In doing so, he knocked the security guard to the side. Mackenzie was so distracted by that, she didn't see the blow coming. Eric Connor threw a lazy punch that connected but hardly hurt. Apparently, his vicious streak stopped at strangling helpless women who were enamored with his level of power.

Mackenzie reeled her arm back, fully prepared to exchange blows with him, but the crowd erupted around her. In the frenzy, she saw a lunging shape come in from the right and recognized the face. It was Ellington—and he was tackling Connor to the ground.

Security came charging for Ellington, but he managed to get his badge and ID out before they could attack. Cameras flashed like lightning and every camera in the place—Mackenzie saw four of them now—was on the sight of Senator Eric Connor being arrested.

"What the hell is this all about?"

The question was loud, raised above the din of the hundred or so people who were now watching as Ellington slapped a pair of handcuffs on Eric Connor. It came from Bruce Dumfries, who looked both scared and somehow relieved all at once.

Mackenzie showed her ID as she turned to him. As calmly as she could, she said, "If you can answer a few questions for us, you'll make that question a lot easier to answer."

And then, as if she needed any further evidence that Connor was guilty, he started to scream and thrash in a rage beneath Ellington. But within seconds, those screams morphed into laughter and it was easily one of the most terrible things Mackenzie had ever heard.

Still, through the laughter, the anger remained. She saw it shining in his eyes as he looked toward the cameras. And there, in front of the cameras and those in attendance, Eric Connor dropped his guard for perhaps the first time in his career, and let his madness show.

CHAPTER TWENTY SEVEN

As she had expected, McGrath was furious. When they arrived at FBI headquarters with Connor in tow half an hour later, McGrath was waiting outside. When Mackenzie opened the car door, he was right there, in her face.

"I'm doing my best to remain as professional as possible and trying to understand that it's not polite to be cruel to a pregnant woman, but I might just have you fired for this." He then looked over the hood of the car at Ellington and said: "And you…you were tagging right along with her. Do you not give a shit about your career?"

"I do, sir. But with all due respect, we're bringing a killer of three women directly to the door of the bureau. I understand your anger, but let's focus on the results first."

Mackenzie had to bite back a grin. She wasn't sure she'd ever heard Ellington stand up to McGrath like this.

McGrath nodded, his hands on his hips. He peered into the back of the car where Eric Connor appeared surprisingly calm, looking out at the confrontation.

"I hope to God you're right," McGrath said. "Because if you're wrong, you've screwed us all." He leveled a finger at Mackenzie, like a teacher calling out an inept student. "I want you in my office as soon as this shit show is over. Am I understood?"

Mackenzie only nodded. McGrath wheeled around and stalked back toward the building, as if he was afraid to be there when they took Connor out of the car. Mackenzie looked back to Connor and saw that he was smiling at what he had just heard. He was gloating, letting them know that he was fully aware how much trouble they could potentially be in. He was no longer making any attempt to seem to be the prestigious and well-respected senator the world had known him as an hour ago.

"Let's get him inside," Ellington said. "Might as well jump out of the frying pan and into the fire while we've still got the nerves."

And the jobs, Mackenzie thought with a hint of worry.

***

Connor was processed and carried back to an interrogation room, where he sat in solitude for almost half an hour before anyone spoke to him. The first words he spoke were to request a call to his lawyers. Meanwhile, outside of headquarters, the street had been cordoned off by the police due to the massive media presence. Reporters, cameramen, and journalists were jockeying for the best position, questioning anyone that came out of the doors for a tidbit on the quickly developing Eric Connor story.

McGrath was the first man in the interrogation room, trying to get a word out of Connor. But Mackenzie watched through the video feed and saw that Connor had no interest in talking. After McGrath had given it a go for nearly fifteen minutes, Connor finally said something. And it was clear by the expression on McGrath's face that it was not what he had wanted to hear.

"I want to talk to Agent White," he said. He then pointed to the camera mounted in the corner and added: "And I want that off. And not a word until my lawyers get here."

"You're not in any condition to be giving demands," McGrath said.

"I was tackled and accused of three murders on live television. And so far, you have presented me with no proof of these crimes. So I actually think I'm in a very *good* position."

The smug smile on Connor's face made it quite clear that he knew how the system worked. He knew that if he was indeed the primary suspect, they'd basically give him whatever he wanted if it meant he'd talk. McGrath stood his ground for another thirty seconds or so before storming out of the room.

He came into the small viewing room where Mackenzie and Ellington had been watching. He looked pissed off but there was also a small inkling of relief on his face. It was an odd combination, but Mackenzie knew it for what it was. He was angry that Connor was being so defiant, but he also knew that he had their man. And there was something about this demeanor—something that had shifted in the man's posture and expression between the time they took him down at the conference and the moment they had taken him out of the car and into FBI headquarters.

"You heard him," McGrath said, sitting down next to her. "He wants you. Probably some bullshit thing about respecting you because you figured him out. And he wants the camera off."

"How much longer before his lawyers get here?"

"Who knows? Soon, I'd think. A story like this one, with all that media out there…that's a lawyer's wet dream."

Sure enough, not one but two lawyers arrived six minutes later while Mackenzie was standing outside of the interrogation room. One of them went directly into the room, escorted by another agent. The other stayed outside and did his best to speak with Mackenzie.

"Our client is being accused of murder, is that correct?"

"Three of them."

The lawyer frowned and looked to his feet for a moment. "Has he spoken with you yet?"

"No. I'm about to go in now that you're here."

"Understood. Give us five minutes with him, would you?"

"No. I've waited long enough."

With that, Mackenzie shouldered past the lawyer. The expression on his face made it clear that he was not used to being treated in such a way.

"Agent White, I advise you—" the lawyer started.

But she ignored him for the time being. She walked directly through the doorway and into the room where Connor sat calmly at a small table while the other lawyer and the agent escort stood to either side. The other agent nodded to Mackenzie and left the room fairly quickly.

The second lawyer entered behind Mackenzie and basically sprinted to the other side of the table so he could whisper something into Connor's ear. Whatever he said made Connor smile, though he never took his eyes off of Mackenzie the entire time. His head was cocked to the side and his eyes narrowed. It seemed like he was trying to figure her out—trying to understand how someone who looked so small and insignificant could have figured him out.

Or he was just trying to intimidate her.

"I hear you wanted to speak with me," Mackenzie said.

He remained quiet for a moment, still looking at her. Mackenzie tried to determine how she needed to respond to this. Should she remain standing and really grill him, or would he respond better to a seated woman that seemed to really not be all that affected by him? Deciding that there were pros and cons of equal measure to both approaches, Mackenzie did what she felt might get a rise out of him—but would also put the lawyers at ease. She sat down directly across from Connor with a slight slouch to her posture. She wanted him to think that she wasn't intimidated by him at all.

"Proud of yourself?" Connor asked.

"Proud?"

"That you figured me out. Not only that, but that you weren't afraid to come after me."

Both lawyers looked as if a bomb had exploded in the room. One of them literally stepped backward, as if unsure how to handle Connor's remark.

"Senator, you need to watch what you say," he said. "This is—"

"This is truth," Connor said, still staring Mackenzie down. "This is life, this is real. I had a very good run." He chuckled at this and when he did, Mackenzie thought she could see something in his eyes, some faraway darkness she had seen in the eyes of other killers.

"So you killed these three women?" Mackenzie asked.

"I said no such thing."

"Did you plan on having Dumfries play the role of scapegoat again?" she asked. "The way he did with the prostitutes?"

"Ah, you must think you're brilliant. Yes…Dumfries has earned every cent I've paid him."

In the back of her head, one red flag started to wave. If Connor was indeed the killer, why were Earl Jackson and his partner called to the Dumfries residence to tend to Dumfries's wife after he had beaten her so badly?

She shrugged and said, "No, not brilliant. If I were brilliant, I would have started looking at you the moment I knew there was someone linked to Humphrey."

"Yes…Humphrey. What a joke. Of course…one of the things you quickly learn in politics is that if you surround yourself with enough shit, you can often come out smelling like a rose."

"Did you murder those women?"

He was quiet, smirking at her.

"Did Dumfries work with you on it?" she asked. "Was he the killer or at least an accomplice of some kind?"

Still, nothing. It was the first lawyer who finally responded. "You can't egregiously make such claims about our client, Agent White. Not without proof."

"A man of your stature," Mackenzie said, looking him dead in the eye. "I figured you'd *want* to talk my ear off to make sure you walk out of here."

"Oh, Agent White…this is not the first time I've felt the FBI breathing down my neck. But money is a very powerful tool. Almost as powerful as influence."

"And that's what it was about for you, right? Power?"

He smiled and looked over his right shoulder. "You're forgetting one of my stipulations for talking, Agent White."

She followed his gaze and saw the camera in the corner. She got up right away and walked over to it. She unscrewed the cable that fed into the main feed that was showing the footage in the interrogation room.

"There you go," she said. "Now, why don't we get the suits out of here, too? I scratched your back…"

Connor considered this for a moment. That evil smile was still on his face as he nodded and waved the lawyers away.

"Senator, I strongly advise—"

"Piss off," Connor said. "Both of you. Go home. You're not needed here."

Mackenzie did her best not to show her hand. But the fact that Connor had essentially stalled in waiting for the lawyers to get here and was now dismissing them to engage in a more honest conversation about the murders…it did not paint a promising outcome for him. It also indicated that there might be some sort of power trip being played out even in this—in not needing someone to represent him as he considered spilling all of his darker deeds.

The lawyers looked at one another, clearly disgusted with the situation. As they made their exit, one of them looked at Connor with absolute befuddlement on his face.

Once the door was closed behind the second lawyer and it was just Mackenzie and Connor, the senator leaned forward and sighed deeply.

"You mentioned power, and you were right," he said. He spoke as if speaking to a very dumb child, having to explain everything, to spell everything out. "It *is* about power. But I don't think I understood that until very recently. I thought control and power were more or less the same thing. Most stuffy assholes in Washington think that way. But I was wrong."

"Took you three deceased women to figure that out?" Mackenzie asked. "Sounds like you're a slow learner."

"Are you trying to make fun of me, Agent White?"

"Not at all. You've killed three women. Killed them after doing God knows what to them just to feel like a big strong man. I find nothing about that funny. I find it pathetic and sad."

"I'm sure you do. But I know a thing or two about creating profiles on people as well. And I know you, Agent White. You stopped at nothing to get to me. You knew it could mean your career, and you came after me. It shows perseverance. It shows a bit of recklessness. And I know those traits lead to one other damning quality…the need to know *why*."

The smile she flashed him was both a little evil and genuine. "Six months ago, you'd be right. But now, I have new things to worry about. I have a new perspective. And while figuring out your need and hunger for power and control *did* help me narrow the suspects down to you, I honestly don't give a shit why you did it."

"Of course you do," Connor argued. "Would you rather hear about my obsession and borderline addiction with sex from an early age? Or the night I listened from my bedroom while my uncle raped my mother and nearly beat her to death? And how I was sort of *glad* he'd done it?"

"You can save that for your shrink," she said. "Because if you're looking for sympathy from me, you're wasting your time."

"I don't want your sympathy. I want someone to share this secret with."

"What secret?"

He smiled wider now and looked as if he were slipping into some sort of ecstasy. "The things I just told you were true...about my uncle, my mother, and the neighbor. And those things, they are quite clear in my head and I go back to them from time to time. But these things I have done...for more than fifteen years now...I don't do them because I was warped by those moments. I do these things because I *like to do it*. Not the reason a shrink would want to hear— or even you, I suppose—but it's the truth. I love to do it. I love to see the look in their eyes when they realize that the little trysts and quickies in the afternoons have become something more dangerous...that I was setting them up from the start."

"I call bullshit," Mackenzie said. "You got cautious there at the end. Trying to dispose of Marie Totino. Not having sex with Christine Lynch before you killed her."

He cocked his head again, as if studying an insect. She could see that darkness looming in his eyes again. It was like watching someone slowly fall asleep as it sparkled in his eyes.

"You like power, too," he commented. "Tracking down the bad guys, trying to understand why they do the things they do."

"That's a different sort of power."

"Is it?" he said through a laugh. "You truly think so? Well...tell me this. If you had to choose between getting a confession out of me or saving a life...which would you choose?"

"What do you mean?" she asked, getting a very bad feeling.

"The longer you keep me here, chatting with me, the chances of there being a fourth go up substantially."

It was the first thing he'd said that she actually cared about. And given the man's current state and the profile that he so snuggly fit into, she doubted he was lying.

"What's that supposed to mean?"

"It means there were four women. Four women that I had chosen to send out of this life before I...*retired,* let's say..."

"They were all at the event last summer?"

"Oh yes. What a night that was. That's how I met them all. All four of them."

"I need a name."

"I think not. You found out Dumfries and then, when it mattered most, saw through that and realized it was me. I do admit that took some fortitude and exceptional smarts. Surely you and your FBI help can figure out who and where this fourth woman is."

"Think about it, Senator. You can go to trial for the murder of three women or four. You're screwed either way, but one is obviously worse than the other."

"You haven't gotten a confession." He looked back to the camera and smiled. "Not a recorded one, anyway."

She had one move left but she wanted to hold on to it. Slowly, she got to her feet and walked to the side of the table. She was within touching distance of him now. If his hands had not been handcuffed, he could have easily reached out and grabbed her.

"Let me share something with you," she said. "I know you sent men to my room to bully me. To beat me up or scare me. But I sent them back to you, limping and wounded. I take some pride in that. But what you *don't know* is that one of your goons kicked me quite hard in the stomach. A stomach that, as of right now, is harboring a sixteen-week-old baby."

An expression somewhere between surprise and delight crossed his face. It took everything in her not to smash his face in.

"Confess to that, at least. You sent them, didn't you?"

"I have no idea what you're talking about. And honestly, it's to my disappointment that he didn't kick harder."

An electric surge passed through her body and she could feel her hand balling into a fist. She got up from the table and walked away as quickly as she could before her emotions got the best of her. She collected herself and slowly walked back to him, reaching into her pocket and taking out her phone. She opened up the voice and set the phone on the table, pressing Play as she did so.

Connor's own voice came back to them, something he'd said about two hours ago.

"...the conference kicks back up. Now, which of you fine folks would like to ask the first question?"

She then pointed to the length of the track, a recording she had ended just fifteen seconds ago.

"I got my confession," she said. "This has been recording ever since I approached you at the conference. Now...taking that into consideration, why don't you tell me where that fourth woman is?"

Connor stared at her with what was easily the most hatred she had ever seen in a gaze. "No," he said. "Your little invasion of privacy just cost that poor woman her life."

"So that'll be four counts of murder," Mackenzie said.

He shrugged, as if indifferent. Again, that smile appeared on his face. "I'm a sporting man, I believe. You want to find that fourth woman?"

"Of course I do."

"I'll tell you where to start. But I want these damned handcuffs taken off of me."

"No way."

"The it seems that fourth murder will be on *your* hands. Not mine."

She had to leave the room. If she stayed there any longer, she'd assault the prick. So with that, she left the room. She found Ellington and McGrath standing outside the door. McGrath looked concerned and a little angry.

"He says there's a fourth one," Mackenzie said. "A fourth victim. He indicated that she's not dead yet but he has her somehow."

"You sure?" Ellington said. "You don't think he's lying?"

"No. He likes bragging too much to be lying. He says he'll give us a starting point to look for her if someone takes off his cuffs."

"Ah, hell...what do you think?" McGrath asked. "Would he really give us legit information?"

"Based on what I can tell...probably. It's just another way for him to show he has us in the palm of his hand. But if it means we save a woman's life, I'm fine with that."

"Ellington...get two officers to go in there. Have one of them uncuff him but *only* after he gives Mackenzie the location."

"One more thing," Mackenzie said, handing her cell phone to McGrath. "It's not exactly a confession, but there's enough to convict on there. Listen to the last five minutes or so. And see if he'll give Ellington the location."

"Why? Where are you going?"

146

Her stomach was already clenching from the surge of emotion and nerves. For a moment, she was afraid she wouldn't make it to the bathroom. Without answering McGrath, she darted down the hallway, praying she would make it in time.

CHAPTER TWENTY EIGHT

While she was washing her hands, her nerves seemed to catch up to everything that had occurred in the last hour or so. She felt it gathering in her stomach and the baby apparently did not like it—which was apparently what had sent her running to the restroom in the first place. Shew tried to fight off the urge but before she knew it, she was throwing up into the sink. Again.

I don't remember reading about this sort of thing in any of those pregnancy books, she thought idly.

When she had control of herself, she then rinsed her mouth out with water from the tap and tried to seem as composed as possible when she stepped back out into the hallway. She made it no more than three steps before she heard her name being barked from behind her.

"White!"

She turned and saw McGrath storming toward her. She noticed that he was looking at the floor, apparently also trying to look composed. Still unable to look at her just yet, he handed her cell phone over to her and a furious nod.

"You're right. There's no confession. But there should be enough to start convicting. And if he's not lying about this fourth woman...just *finding* her would be a step towards prosecution. Also...on that recording, you mention to Connor that six months ago, you would have handled something differently. I want you to think about that. I want you to think about how you might have handled this entire case differently if you weren't pregnant."

It felt almost sexist for him to say such a thing but she knew what he meant. And he was right.

"He still hasn't asked for his lawyers to return," McGrath said. "It makes me think he's just accepting it. He's giving up."

"Yeah, me too. And it makes no sense. He enjoys being in control. Why would he stop now?"

"He does mention retiring in the recording—even if he *was* using it ironically."

That could be it, but Mackenzie thought she had another answer. Connor knew that he was no longer in control—that any semblance of power was out of his reach. Maybe it would have been different if Mackenzie had not revealed the recording to him. But for now, he knew he had lost control. And without control, what was the point in carrying on?

Before McGrath could offer any sort of opinion, they both heard footfalls marching down the hallway. They looked to the left, where Ellington was approaching from one of the other interrogation rooms, flanked by two police officers.

"He gave us a vague location," Ellington said. "Spilled the beans on a ton of things after that, though, as soon as we uncuffed him. Still spilling to some of the police, actually. But for right now, I think we've got what we need. There's a secondary living space, about eight miles away from Queen Nash. An apartment. We don't know anything else for sure. No address, no apartment number, nothing. Just that he would take women there sometimes."

"I want you up there," McGrath said. He then looked to the police officers and asked: "Can we get an escort?"

"Absolutely."

"In the meantime, call the Baltimore PD and have them narrow this search down. If they can find her before Ellington even gets on the scene, that would be perfect."

"One apartment about eight miles away from campus," Mackenzie said. "That narrows it down, but that's still a needle in a haystack."

"I'll make sure the police give every available mind over to this one. Landlords, noise complaints, anything worth looking into."

Ellington nodded as he started to rush for the end of the hallway, toward the front of the building. Mackenzie followed along, the two officers running between them.

"Agent White," McGrath said. "Where the hell do you think you're going?"

When she turned toward him, she didn't try too hard to hide the sorrow in her eyes. She'd been expecting resistance from him and was ready to go down fighting.

"I got your suspect. We got a potential location for the fourth victim. In the last five days, I've seen two dead women, abused and neglected. Please, sir…let me find this one alive. I have to…I have to help find this one alive."

She could tell that McGrath was struggling between protocol and a calling to do the right thing. Finally, with a sigh and a grimace, he nodded. "Go. But if it goes *anywhere* beyond simply finding this woman, you keep your ass away from the action. Am I understood?"

"Loud and clear," she said.

She turned away from him before the tear came trickling out of the corner of her eye. And with her back to him, she ran quickly down the hall to catch up with Ellington and the two police officers.

***

True to his word, McGrath had set as many people on the task of narrowing down the address as possible. During the thirty-three-minute car ride to Baltimore, he had managed to come up with sixteen potential apartments to look into. It was all based on records, landlord grievances, and any call about negligent or disorderly conduct. He'd also set his feelers out for apartments that were paid for on a recurring basis without the tenant actually sending in checks or money. This, plus asking for apartments where the landlord knew that resident rarely lived at the residence, made the search a little more bearable.

Meanwhile, McGrath had set Yardley and Harrison on a track to expedite some the less-stressed details such as re-interviewing people who had last seen Jo Haley, Christine Lynch, and Marie Totino. Harrison, specifically, was speaking with a liaison from Marie's cell phone carrier, trying to determine her last location, and local PD in trying to locate her car. These were tasks that had, of course, been on their radar but tended to take some time.

"You know McGrath is going to have your ass for continually pushing on this, right?" Ellington asked.

"Yet he keeps giving me slack…keeps saying yes." She had to say it because, honestly, she was pretty sure her husband was right.

"That's because respects you more than you think and—"

He was interrupted by Mackenzie's phone ringing. She had been fielding calls for the duration of the trip while Ellington drove. It was infuriating but also gave the case the feeling that it was finally headed somewhere. They had the killer and now they were on the trail to hopefully save a potential fourth victim. And they were speeding toward a conclusion at nearly one hundred miles per hour.

Mackenzie answered the call, hoping it would be the call that would lead them to the fourth victim. "This is Agent White," she said.

"Hey, White. It's Harrison."

"Tell me you've got something good."

"I think I might. You in the city yet?"

"About to get off on the west side. Why?"

"Don't," he said. "Skip it and go two exits up."

"Why? You got an address?"

"Maybe. I wanted you two to have a crack at it first. I just got off of the phone with Marie Totino's cell phone service provider. They indicate that her phone has been in the same spot for fifty-nine hours. And it *is* exactly eight miles away from Queen Nash."

"Are you and Yardley headed to the location?"

"We are, but we're coming from Bethesda, where we were pushing the DMV around. Based on this address, you'll get there before us."

"Give it to me."

He did, and she recited it to Ellington. Based on the address alone, she was fairly certain the phone had not been discarded in the river when Connor disposed of the body. Maybe it was in Marie's car. Or even better still, in the apartment Connor had lured her to.

"Thanks, Harrison. Do you mind calling the State PD to let them know? Every second counts here, so if they can get there before us…"

"Yeah, I'm on it."

Mackenzie ended the call and, in that lovely mind-to-mind communication that she and Ellington were starting to develop, he recited the address to her without having to be asked. She plugged it into her GPS as one of the exits Harrison had indicated blazed by them. The coordinates came up, and she found herself leaning forward in anticipation.

"Take the next exit," she said. "We're less than three miles away from the location of Marie's phone."

Ellington stepped on the gas, blasting the car to one hundred as the exit came into view. Mackenzie, meanwhile, got on the phone and contacted their escort officers to fill them on what was going on.

Whether it was the excitement of closing the case, finding the fourth victim before it was too late, or the speed that Ellington was driving, Mackenzie wasn't sure…but her stomach started to do that all-too-familiar surge and roll.

No, baby. Not right now, please…

She took a series of deep breaths and grasped the door handle, trying to steady herself. She closed her eyes as Ellington took the exit, the tires screeching. Ahead of them, their police escorts tuned on the sirens to accompany the lights.

Almost done, baby, Mackenzie said, trying to ease the nausea. *Give Mommy fifteen more minutes, what do you say?*

She couldn't help but smile as the sensations slowly passed. She opened her eyes and looked at the GPS. They were now just 1.2

miles away from the address Harrison had given them. As they closed in, she picked the phone back up and called McGrath.

"You talk to Harrison yet?" he asked.

"I did," Mackenzie answered. "We're a mile away. You got any apartment listings from your hunt that relate to that address?"

"I've got someone on the phone with the landlord now. Stand by and I'll let you know."

She did that as Ellington tore through a red light, the escorts leading the way.

For Mackenzie, it was bittersweet. They seemed to be closing in on a woman who was likely going to be Connor's fourth victim. And while the idea of rescuing her and hopefully mining enough information out of her to put Connor away for life was exciting, Mackenzie also knew that it might very well be the last case she was actively a part of until the baby came. And when she added that amount of time to the amount of time she'd need to recuperate and take maternity leave, she was looking at about eight or nine months.

Yes, the prospect of becoming a mother was becoming more and more important to her, but was she ready to put that above her career? It was something she had never been asked to do, not even with Ellington and their relationship.

It was a scary thought and one that she tried not to let bog her down as Ellington brought the car around a hard right turn, finally bringing them to their destination.

Ellington wasted no time looking for a parking spot. He brought the car to a skidding halt at the far end of the lot where he blocked in two other cars. They both hurried out of the car, drawing their weapons in unison.

Mackenzie and Ellington had barely made it to the sidewalk that ran along the front of the apartment building before a police cruiser came tearing into the parking lot. She could hear more sirens in the distance as more cruisers responded to the call. The officers got out of the car but stopped when they saw the agents entering the building.

"What can we do to help?" one of them shouted over the top of the car.

"Check the plates on every car in this parking lot. See if you can locate the cars of any of our three victims. We know for a fact that Marie Totino's cell phone is somewhere on the premises. Maybe it's in her car."

She and Ellington then stepped inside the building. The front lobby was dimly lit and the building looked like any number of lower-income apartment buildings. The walls could have used a fresh coat of paint, the elevator doors were marred in graffiti, and there was a strong aroma of astringent cleaner that had not done its job to the fullest extent.

"What if this isn't him?" Ellington asked as they started for the stairs, still with no clear indication as to which apartment to check.

"Then we start over," she said. "We check Christine's phone...Jo's phone..."

But in her heart of hearts, she felt that this was it. Even though they had no apartment to start checking, she had a feeling deep in her bones that they were in the right place.

As if summoned by Mackenzie's purely positive thoughts, her phone rang. She barely took the time to register that it was McGrath before answering it. "What apartment?" she asked.

"I've got two for you to check. Apartment twenty-seven is leased by a tenant that several people have complained about. Noisy at night, the smell of marijuana permeating the hallway coming from his door."

"That wouldn't be it," she said. Someone like Connor would not live in a place like this. No, this was his lair...his nest. This was where he brought the women so that no one would catch him—a place far enough away from campus to create distance but close enough to still maintain the campus as a hunting ground for women starving to get a career started. To learn about control and power...

"Apartment thirty-three has been rented out for several years and the landlord says he's only ever met the guy once. Rent shows up in the mail right on time every month, always cash. He says he doesn't have any record of mail delivery for that apartment."

"Thirty-three," Mackenzie said to Ellington.

She hung up on McGrath as she and Ellington bounded up the stairs while the sound of even more approaching sirens filled the world outside.

***

Apartment number thirty-three was, of course, locked. Mackenzie stepped aside to allow Ellington room to take one stride back toward the wall before he delivered a vicious kick to the side of the door just beneath the knob. The first attack only splintered the frame and loosened the knob. With a grunt of frustration, Ellington backed up once more. This time he threw his shoulder into it, nearly diving into the door shoulder-first.

The door blasted open, the blow so hard that the top hinge popped loose and went clattering to the floor. With the door knocked down, Mackenzie strode in behind Ellington. The doorway led into a small kitchen area which was directly linked to a living room, separated only by a small bar area.

"Hello?" Mackenzie called. "Is there anyone here?"

Only silence greeted them. They stood absolutely still, listening for the sound again.

"Hello?" Mackenzie said again, louder this time.

The returning silence was unnerving. They started to investigate the place, starting in the living room and then splitting up to check the rest of the place. It was sparsely furnished, with only a couch and a coffee table in the living area.

Makes sense, if he's only using it to bring women back to have sex with them...or kill them, Mackenzie thought.

Mackenzie checked the one bedroom while Ellington looked into the small office space off of the living room. The bedroom looked like a place someone might squat in, with nothing but a bare mattress on the floor and dark curtains over the windows. She checked the closet and found it just as desolate.

She walked out of the bedroom and started down the hallway. She came to a door that she assumed would either lead to the bathroom or another closet. She opened it up and instantly stepped back at what she saw inside.

There was a woman in the closet. She was naked and hanging by handcuffs from a steel runner that ran the length of the closet—a runner that was, in a more traditional sense, used to hang clothes from. Her mouth was taped up by several layers of black electrical tape, a few of the strands wrapping all the way around the lower part of her head. It looked as if her left shoulder was out of socket, the arm bent back at a sick angle away from the rest of her body while it was forcibly pulled up by the handcuffs.

There were a few bruises on her body and a thin river of dried blood on the side of her face. The two worst bruises were located directly above her breast and along most of her neck.

The woman's head hung down low. Her chest did not rise and fall, and she did not make a single sound.

They were too late.

The woman was dead.

"Babe..." she said. It was probably the first time she had referred to Ellington in such a way while on the job. But in that moment, she was not aware of it. Her heart was breaking and a cauldron of sheer hatred and animosity started to bubble in her guts.

Ellington came rushing in her direction. When his eyes fell on the woman in the closet, he let out a little gasp and then wrapped an arm around Mackenzie.

"He knew she'd be dead," Ellington said. "Or he maybe even already knew she was dead. This is not our fault. We couldn't have gotten here in time. There's no way we could have known."

In her heart, Mackenzie knew he was right. But that anger in her stomach was radiating out, causing her to tremble. She was so angry and overcome with emotion that when tears started to spill out of her eyes, it only enraged her further.

"Come on," Ellington said, guiding her away from the closet. "Let's get the cops in on this. You need to rest. You need to get away from this."

She allowed herself to be led away from the sight of the body in the closet. She wondered how long the poor woman had been hanging there before she died. She wondered if she had died from external injuries, starvation, maybe something else.

But she pushed all of those questions away. She allowed them to drift off to be answered later. For right now, she focused all of her attention on a man who sat in an interrogation room about half an hour away.

He would be free of his handcuffs thanks to his little tip, and as Ellington had suggested, he had likely known this fourth woman was dead.

The idea that he had indeed been in control after all stoked the fires of her hate and despite the overwhelming emotion Mackenzie could not wait to be face to face with him again.

CHAPTER TWENTY NINE

An hour and a half later, Mackenzie was standing in a conference room just two doors way from the interrogation room that contained Eric Connor. To one side, there was Ellington. He was holding her hand and looking at her in a way that made her feel beyond loved. Sitting at the table with a notepad in his hand and a scowl on his face was McGrath.

"In the time you've been gone, he's said only one thing. Every time someone tries to engage him in conversation, he says the same thing. 'I'm waiting on Agent White.' And that's all we get out of him."

"It's his last grasp of control," she said. "I don't know why he essentially confessed without much grilling...maybe because he wanted to flaunt it in front of us. *Look what I got away with...your failings cost the lives of four women.* Demanding to speak to me and no one else is just him trying to maintain control."

"You don't have to speak with him," Ellington said. "We've got your recording plus the fact that he told us a general location of where the fourth woman was. It's enough to convict. It'll be a long trial with lots of ins and outs, but I think it would be enough."

"I agree," McGrath said. "Agent White, this is your call."

"I'll talk to him," she said. "If nothing else, it will be closure for me."

McGrath nodded, not bothering to argue. Mackenzie figured he'd been expecting as much. "We'll be right outside the door. If you can get a verbal confession out of him, that's preferable. If not...don't push too hard. You've done more than enough...more than I've been comfortable with, if I'm being honest."

Ellington reached out and took her hand. "Are you sure? You owe him nothing. I don't want you playing into his hands."

"I'm sure."

"I'm at least sending a policeman in there with you," McGrath said.

Mackenzie didn't think it was necessary, but she didn't bother arguing. Without another word, she exited the conference room and headed down the hallway to the interrogation room. She didn't pause before entering or make any sort of dramatic entrance. She

156

simply entered the room as if she were a causal visitor. A uniformed cop came rushing in behind her at McGrath's urging. The cop closed the door behind them as Mackenzie settled in to the seat opposite Eric Connor.

"The woman was ID'ed as Bridgette Minkus," Mackenzie said. "We found her dead, hanging from her wrists in your closet."

Connor seemed a little surprised by this. He shifted uncomfortably in his seat. The police officer, maybe not liking the tension, moved slightly behind Connor so that he was covered from the front by Mackenzie and from the back by himself. In that moment, Mackenzie noted that Connor's hands were still uncuffed from having made his little deal with Ellington.

"You look surprised," Mackenzie said. "Did you not think we'd find her so soon? You know...for someone who craves control, smaller details escape you pretty easily. Marie Totino's car in the parking lot of the building, for instance. And her cell phone, right there in the center console."

"I figured she'd be dead," Connor said nonchalantly. "She was quite weak when I checked in on her this morning. I planned to get rid of her this afternoon, after the conference."

"Did Dumfries help with that sort of detail, too?"

"No. He hasn't helped me in things like this for a while. I believe the only reason he remained loyal to me was because of some dirt I had on him. Dirt involving his wife."

"The calls to his residence...the ones your bodyguards helped clean up..."

"Those were my messes. Dumfries was very understanding. He knew his wife and I were having an affair. And when she wanted out...well, I didn't like that. But Dumfries chose his career over his wife. He took the fall."

This guy is deluded and deranged, Mackenzie thought. *And very dangerous. Crazy, maybe.*

"You haven't given an actual confession," Mackenzie said. "But we have enough small crumbs to take this to court. My recording, you giving us the general whereabouts of the fourth body. If Dumfries is at all involved in this, now is the time to tell us."

"No. Dumfries never killed anyone. He does have quite the love for ladies of the night. But...if you're going to arrest everyone that has that craving within DC, you'll pack this place out."

"You led me to a dead woman, knowing she'd likely be dead when we got there," Mackenzie said. "I know you think that was your way of stringing us along—of keeping your position of power and control. But that's over now. When I step out of this room, you won't speak with me again. So if you have anything else to say, now is the time."

"You think I *don't* have control? You think I'm powerless? I've had you and your friends running in circles...going after idiots like Humphrey and Dumfries. And why? Because even I know that your precious bureau is hesitant to go after senators. Too much money and red tape involved. Agent White...I've been in control of this situation before you even attended the academy, I guarantee it. And I will maintain control of this entire case."

"If you say so," Mackenzie said.

"Oh, I do. And I feel that you won't even get to see me go down. Because I won't let that happen."

"You truly are delusional," she said.

Done with this nonsense, she got up from her chair, anxious to be away from the power-hungry maniac. As she turned her back, she heard a commotion from behind her. She was fully expecting to see Connor scrambling over the table for her when she turned around, but she saw something entirely different and unexpected.

Connor had driven his elbow into the stomach of the cop behind him. As Mackenzie's eyes fell on the scene, Connor's hand was freeing the cop's gun from his holster. The cop fought back, but it was too late. By the time the cop had his hand wrapped around Connor's arm, Connor had positioned the gun in the way he needed.

It was not aimed at Mackenzie, but at himself.

Still, when he pulled the trigger, Mackenzie fully expected the bullet to come for her, passing through her heart or head.

She did not truly feel free from the threat of it until the aftermath sank in.

The cop fell to the ground with a scream. But based on the rest of what she saw, she didn't think he had actually been hurt.

Connor hadn't had time to properly position the gun, so it had gone in through his jaw at an upward angle rather than through the bottom of his chin. Still, the effect had been equally effective and gruesome. He collapsed in the chair, falling out in a dead heap as blood cascaded out of his head and onto the floor.

"Mackenzie!"

The door came flying open and Ellington practically dove toward her. McGrath came in behind him, his gun drawn. After he took in the situation, he went to the fallen officer. He had not been shot, but his face was covered in the gore of Connor's shot.

Mac...Mac..." Ellington said, taking her in his arms.

Behind them, more policemen rushed into the room. And even though the entire ordeal was now over—their suspect dead on the floor by his own hand—one thing occurred to Mackenzie that chilled her to the core.

In ending his own life in the wake of a near-confession, Eric Connor left the world on his own terms—and in control of his fate.

CHAPTER THIRTY

Three days later, Mackenzie was waiting in McGrath's reception area. She was alone, as Ellington was working with Yardley and Harrison on finalizing the full list of charges that would officially be brought against Eric Connor in the weeks to come. And because McGrath's secretary wasn't even at work yet, the place was dead quiet.

When she heard the elevator ping open from the doorway, she figured it was McGrath. He'd wanted her here early, wanted to make sure they didn't have any distractions that might come up during the day to interfere with being able to meet. Secretly, though, Mackenzie was worried that he had planned it so early in the morning so that she would not be able to put any hours in—that he fully intended to suspend her.

Sure enough, McGrath came into the reception area a few seconds later. He had a coffee in one hand and his briefcase in the other. He looked to be in a good mood, his face not pulled slightly down in that permanent sneer he seemed to always wear.

"Good morning, White. Come on in."

He unlocked his office and went directly behind his desk, where he started to set up his workspace. Mackenzie settled into her usual chair—the chair that always made her feel as if she was visiting the principal's office.

"Did you hear the news?" he asked.

"Doubtful. I've sort of been zoned out and doing nothing these last three days."

"There is a huge push for Neil Rooney to fill in for Eric Connor. As of right now, the slot is vacant. And while I honestly don't know all of the rules and legislation, it looks like he's going to get it. There will be a vote, of course, but based on the excellent way he's handled himself in the last few days based on what happened with Connor, he's almost certain to get it. And if it goes well there, this is not just Rooney getting his foot in the door of higher political offices—this is Rooney basically tearing every damned door down."

"That's good, right? It seems he's a stand-up guy."

"Seems that way. Of course...the vast majority of people thought the same about Connor. Since he died, a few women have come forward and spilled some other details about him. So far we're up to about five cases of rape, one of which included a pregnancy and abortion."

"Any news on Bridgette Minkus?"

"A bit, mostly from family and, believe it not, from Daniel Humphrey, who has all of a sudden become quite helpful. It seems Bridgette had been meeting with Eric Connor off and on for about a year. She met him at a rally here in DC and exchanged numbers. After a while, they became physical. It was just sex and nothing more. That came from some of her friends...and that's about all we have.

"As for Eric Connor...it's not just women coming forward. People like Dumfries are revealing that Connor was making money on deals concerning drug and sex trafficking. He said it was common for Connor to be involved in parties that basically devolved into drug orgies. Dumfries himself has basically been ostracized for having taken part in some of them."

"So this case sort of did some political spring cleaning in other words?"

"It did. And I hate to tell you, but your name is bound to end up in the news as well. For now, the reports are only showcasing that it was a bureau effort. We're trying to keep it quiet but this case has rocked DC. Journalists are going to dig and your name is sure to come up."

"It'll be something to keep me entertained while I'm at home for the next few months, right?" she said.

He smiled and sighed deeply. "About that. Look...I'm honestly not all that upset about you hiding the pregnancy from me. You're stubborn at heart and you love your job. I get why you did it. But, Agent White...the stunt you and Ellington pulled at the conference...not to mention your visit out to Richmond to speak with Earl Jackson...I wish I could say these were things that were very much unlike you. But the fact of the matter is, they are *very* much like you. And I need that to stop. And quite frankly, it *will* stop." He paused here and leaned forward. The sincerity on his face was taking Mackenzie off guard. "How far along are you?" he asked.

"Coming up on seventeen weeks."

"Are you going to find out the sex?"

It was such a friendly question that she had to bite back a smile. "We haven't decided yet."

He smiled and shook his head. "I have to reprimand you, White. Certainly, you know that. So in the interest of sticking to protocol and being a decent human being that realizes you are about to have a baby, here's the deal I have for you. And it is non-negotiable."

"Okay…"

"I want you to finish out the week, helping to put the last pieces of this Eric Connor case to bed. Follow up on all the loose ends you need to. Get it done by Friday. Because effective Monday morning, you're suspended for the duration of your pregnancy. Between the two of us, I have looked all over the books for some way to skew this into an extended maternity leave sort of situation, but there's nothing. Not unless the baby is in danger. And apparently, your baby is as tough as you…so that's not an option."

"Sir, that's almost five months. Can't you at least assign me to research and resource tasks from home?"

"No. It's a suspension, plain and simple. Like I said…non-negotiable."

Mackenzie nodded, trying to make sure she did not cry in front of McGrath. "I understand. Is that all?"

"Yes. You're excused. But…look…good work on this. I was about to fire you on the spot for having us chase after a senator. Typically, that doesn't go well for the bureau. So I'm glad you stuck with your gut. You never fail to impress me, Mackenzie. Don't let this little dent of a suspension get in the way of that."

It was the perfect way to end the meeting. There was nothing more he could say to get his point across, nor to have her in rather high spirits upon leaving his office.

When she left, she didn't bother with a single look back. Like he said…she had a bright future ahead of her, so what was the point in looking back?

As if she needed a reminder of that bright future, her hand instinctually went to her stomach, where the bulge was getting larger.

***

Two nights later, Mackenzie woke up with a gasp coming up out of her throat.

She looked around the bedroom, sure there had been someone there. But of course, the only other person was Ellington, dead asleep beside her.

What woke me up? she wondered. *What was that?*

But then she knew. She knew because she felt it again.

The baby was moving. She'd felt small flutters a few times before, but this was different. It wasn't quite a kick, but it was noticeable movement.

It was probably the strangest thing she had ever felt. It wasn't painful, though it wasn't quite pleasant, either. She waited for it to come again and when it did, it was much smaller this time.

Afraid the baby was going to be done with its little assault any moment now, she reached out and shook Ellington by the shoulder. "Babe...wake up."

"What's it? You okay?" He barely rolled over, his body trying to decide if it was an emergency.

"Wake up. Someone wants to say hello."

"What?"

She took his hand and pulled him closer to her. She then placed it on her stomach and waited. Ellington, apparently sensing what had happened, sat up in bed right away. A smile inched its way across his sleepy features instantly.

And there was the baby again. Mackenzie figured it might be a little knee or perhaps an elbow, as the little edges of a solid shape were clearly felt. Mackenzie let out a little giggle that brought with it a tear or two.

"Oh my God," Ellington said. "That's...that's beautiful. And a little weird."

"*You* think it feels weird?"

He kissed her on the lips, his hand still on her stomach. The baby made its presence known once more before it apparently decided it was done.

"You okay?" Ellington asked her as their hands finally left her stomach.

"Yes," she said. "I'm perfect."

And for the first time since being kicked in the stomach in a hotel room in Baltimore, that was a true statement. Even though she had been without work for five weeks and still had a lengthy stretch to go, she did not care. Because for the first time since seeing that positive result on the pregnancy test, she knew the answer to the question that had been haunting her.

If she had to, would she choose parenthood over her career?

She smiled in the darkness when she realized that it was the easiest *yes* she could imagine.

BEFORE HE ENVIES
(A Mackenzie White Mystery—Book 12)

From Blake Pierce, #1 bestselling author of ONCE GONE (a #1 bestseller with over 1,200 five star reviews), comes BEFORE HE ENVIES, book #12 in the heart-pounding Mackenzie White mystery series.

BEFORE HE ENVIES is book #12 in the bestselling Mackenzie White mystery series, which begins with BEFORE HE KILLS (Book #1), a free download with over 500 five-star reviews!

When two rock climbers turn up dead, each killed in the same disturbing way, FBI Special Agent Mackenzie White, mother of a newborn baby, must face her fear of heights as she is summoned to catch a serial killer before he strikes again.

Mackenzie, settling into motherhood, wants to take some time off. But it is not meant to be. Rock climbers are turning up dead in Colorado, hunted by an elusive serial killer, caught at their most prone moments. A disturbing pattern emerges, and Mackenzie soon realizes she is up against a monster.

And that the only way to catch him will be to enter his diabolical mind.

Feeling the effects of post partum and not ready to return to her job, Mackenzie finds herself ill prepared for the hunt of her life.

A dark psychological thriller with heart-pounding suspense, BEFORE HE ENVIES is book #12 in a riveting new series—with a beloved new character—that will leave you turning pages late into the night.

Blake Pierce

Blake Pierce is author of the bestselling RILEY PAGE mystery series, which includes fifteen books (and counting). Blake Pierce is also the author of the MACKENZIE WHITE mystery series, comprising twelve books (and counting); of the AVERY BLACK mystery series, comprising six books; of the KERI LOCKE mystery series, comprising five books; of the MAKING OF RILEY PAIGE mystery series, comprising three books (and counting); of the KATE WISE mystery series, comprising three books (and counting); of the CHLOE FINE psychological suspense mystery, comprising three books (and counting); and of the JESSE HUNT psychological suspense thriller series, comprising three books (and counting).

An avid reader and lifelong fan of the mystery and thriller genres, Blake loves to hear from you, so please feel free to visit www.blakepierceauthor.com to learn more and stay in touch.

BOOKS BY BLAKE PIERCE

A JESSIE HUNT PSYCHOLOGICAL SUSPENSE SERIES
THE PERFECT WIFE (Book #1)
THE PERFECT BLOCK (Book #2)
THE PERFECT HOUSE (Book #3)

CHLOE FINE PSYCHOLOGICAL SUSPENSE MYSTERY
NEXT DOOR (Book #1)
A NEIGHBOR'S LIE (Book #2)
CUL DE SAC (Book #3)

KATE WISE MYSTERY SERIES
IF SHE KNEW (Book #1)
IF SHE SAW (Book #2)
IF SHE RAN (Book #3)
IF SHE HID (Book #4)

THE MAKING OF RILEY PAIGE SERIES
WATCHING (Book #1)
WAITING (Book #2)
LURING (Book #3)

RILEY PAIGE MYSTERY SERIES
ONCE GONE (Book #1)
ONCE TAKEN (Book #2)
ONCE CRAVED (Book #3)
ONCE LURED (Book #4)
ONCE HUNTED (Book #5)
ONCE PINED (Book #6)
ONCE FORSAKEN (Book #7)
ONCE COLD (Book #8)
ONCE STALKED (Book #9)
ONCE LOST (Book #10)
ONCE BURIED (Book #11)
ONCE BOUND (Book #12)
ONCE TRAPPED (Book #13)
ONCE DORMANT (Book #14)
ONCE SHUNNED (Book #15)

MACKENZIE WHITE MYSTERY SERIES

BEFORE HE KILLS (Book #1)
BEFORE HE SEES (Book #2)
BEFORE HE COVETS (Book #3)
BEFORE HE TAKES (Book #4)
BEFORE HE NEEDS (Book #5)
BEFORE HE FEELS (Book #6)
BEFORE HE SINS (Book #7)
BEFORE HE HUNTS (Book #8)
BEFORE HE PREYS (Book #9)
BEFORE HE LONGS (Book #10)
BEFORE HE LAPSES (Book #11)
BEFORE HE ENVIES (Book #12)

AVERY BLACK MYSTERY SERIES
CAUSE TO KILL (Book #1)
CAUSE TO RUN (Book #2)
CAUSE TO HIDE (Book #3)
CAUSE TO FEAR (Book #4)
CAUSE TO SAVE (Book #5)
CAUSE TO DREAD (Book #6)

KERI LOCKE MYSTERY SERIES
A TRACE OF DEATH (Book #1)
A TRACE OF MUDER (Book #2)
A TRACE OF VICE (Book #3)
A TRACE OF CRIME (Book #4)
A TRACE OF HOPE (Book #5)

43145965R00102

Made in the USA
Middletown, DE
20 April 2019